Alyssa ran toward the woods.

She ignored the pain stabbing through her knee. As she disappeared into the tree line, two shots rang out. One pinged off a tree just ahead, less than two feet to her right.

A cold male voice reached her. "I'll take care of her. You go after the other one."

Her knees almost buckled, and her stomach dropped. They were going after Spencer. He was armed—but was he in any shape to use what he was carrying? Was he even conscious? She had to do something.

Several shots rang out in rapid succession, and she stifled a shriek. Hand pressed over her mouth, she slunk around the tree, keeping it between herself and the man who was hunting her.

She closed her eyes, afraid to even breathe. *Keep going.* If her attacker continued to follow whatever he'd heard, she could double back. Maybe she could get to Spence.

Carol J. Post writes fun and fast-paced inspirational romantic suspense stories and lives in the beautiful mountains of North Carolina. She plays the piano and also enjoys sailing, hiking and camping—almost anything outdoors. Her daughters and grandkids live too far away for her liking, so she now pours all that nurturing into taking care of two highly spoiled black cats.

Books by Carol J. Post

Love Inspired Suspense

Midnight Shadows
Motive for Murder
Out for Justice
Shattered Haven
Hidden Identity
Mistletoe Justice
Buried Memories
Reunited by Danger
Fatal Recall
Lethal Legacy
Bodyguard for Christmas
Dangerous Relations
Trailing a Killer

Canine Defense

Searching for Evidence
Sniffing Out Justice
Uncovering the Truth

Visit the Author Profile page
at LoveInspired.com for more titles.

UNCOVERING THE TRUTH

CAROL J. POST

LOVE INSPIRED SUSPENSE
INSPIRATIONAL ROMANCE

LOVE INSPIRED® SUSPENSE
INSPIRATIONAL ROMANCE

Recycling programs
for this product may
not exist in your area.

ISBN-13: 978-1-335-48401-7

Uncovering the Truth

Love Inspired
22 Adelaide St. West, 41st Floor
Toronto, Ontario M5H 4E3, Canada
www.LoveInspired.com

Printed in U.S.A.

Therefore if any man be in Christ,
he is a new creature: old things are passed away;
behold, all things are become new.
—*2 Corinthians* 5:17

Thank you to my wonderful sister, Kim Coker—
my plotting partner, my research buddy
and my all-time best friend.

Thank you to my editor, Katie Gowrie,
and my critique partners, Karen Fleming and
Sabrina Jarema. Your amazing insight
always makes my writing better.

And lastly, thank you to my husband, Chris, for your
encouragement and support. If I had it to do over,
I would do it all over again.

ONE

The overstuffed backpack landed on the scuffed counter with a thud.

Alyssa Anderson rolled her shoulders and rang the bell. Five minutes later, she was still alone in the motel lobby. Granted, this wasn't the Ritz-Carlton or even a Holiday Inn. But someone ought to at least be manning the front desk.

"Hello?"

Moments later, a young woman came from the back and stepped up to the counter, looking a little harried. "Sorry to keep you waiting. How can I help you?"

"I need a room for the night." Maybe more than one night, depending on how long it would take the mechanic to get to her hunk-of-junk car.

"Sure thing." She made several clicks of the mouse, squinting at the computer screen.

The clock on the wall behind her said almost four thirty. Alyssa shifted her weight to the other foot. Her mother's graveside service would have ended an hour ago. More than a decade had passed since she'd been killed, and she was finally getting a proper burial, her death, the mourning it deserved.

The service had probably been beautiful, with friends and family members remembering a life well lived but cut short. The words spoken over the casket had likely included the 23rd Psalm and other verses of comfort.

Alyssa wouldn't know. She hadn't made it. One more reason for her sisters to judge her.

It wasn't that she hadn't tried. She'd left Atlanta in plenty of time to make the five-hour trip to Pensacola. She'd only gotten as far as LaGrange when the old Tempo had made a sound resembling an explosion and started rattling as if trying to shake off all four fenders.

The clerk straightened and met Alyssa's gaze. "I'll put you in room 106. That'll be $54.88 with tax. How did you want to pay?"

"Debit card." She hesitated. "On second thought, I'll pay cash."

She was probably being overly cautious. Maybe even a bit paranoid. No one had access to her bank account, so there was no way for anyone to follow her trail through her banking transactions.

Regardless, she pulled two twenties, a ten and a five from her wallet and laid them on the counter. If there was anything she'd learned over the past decade, it was how to take care of herself.

After printing a receipt, the clerk slid the room key into its sleeve and wrote 106 on the outside. "Checkout is at eleven."

"Thank you." Alyssa folded the receipt

then palmed the room key and slipped both into the back pocket of her jeans.

She hoped she wouldn't have to extend her stay. Even if the mechanic didn't get her car fixed until late tomorrow, she'd do what she'd done today. After having her car towed, she had spent seven hours riding public transportation, roaming the LaGrange Mall and strolling the park to pass the time until check-in.

She hadn't bothered to call either of her sisters. One of them would have driven from Pensacola to pick her up as soon as the service was over. But she didn't want charity from anyone, least of all her up-pity sisters.

She dragged the backpack from the counter and slid an arm through one of the straps. The pack was remarkably light considering it held all of her worldly pos-sessions. She heaved a sigh. She was pretty pathetic—twenty-five years of life and all she had to show for it fit into a space the size of a carry-on.

After walking out the door, she turned left and made her way along the front of the building. Her room was six doors down.

Her burner phone rang before she'd even made it halfway. She fished it from her pocket and eyed the 706 area code. Her pulse kicked up speed. Maybe the mechanic already knew what was wrong with her car. Now if she could just get it fixed without having to wipe out her entire savings.

Whatever happened, going back to Atlanta wasn't an option, not if she hoped to escape the latest mess she'd gotten herself into. And since her mother's graveside service was over, there was nothing for her in Pensacola. Nothing except a couple of sisters who would probably rather she not return anyway.

She swiped to accept the call and pressed the phone to her ear. She'd guessed right. The call was from Jim's Garage, where they'd towed her car, and the mechanic had already diagnosed her engine troubles. Not only that, he'd fixed them.

"How much do I owe you?"

"Two hundred dollars."

Was that all? She breathed a sigh of relief. The problem had to have been extremely minor. She would call a cab, try to get her money back from the motel clerk, pick up her car and be gone. The sooner she could get out of LaGrange, the better. Actually, the sooner she could leave Georgia behind, the safer she would feel.

When the cab arrived, she walked out of the lobby fifty-five dollars richer than when she'd gone in. A few minutes later, the driver dropped her off at the garage. Her Tempo was parked out front, next to a Chevy Trailblazer. A Nissan pickup waited along the side of the building.

She stepped into the office area where a man sat at a desk that was covered in papers, a phone pressed to his ear. While she waited for him to finish, she glanced through the door leading into the side of the garage. Another man was leaning forward under the open hood of a Chevy pickup truck.

He straightened, and she wandered in. "Are you the one who repaired the red Tempo?"

He closed the hood and pulled a rag from the pocket of his overalls. "That was me."

"So what was wrong with it?"

He wiped his hands on the rag. "You threw a piston rod. It's a good thing it went into the cylinder head instead of out the side of the block or you would have needed a new engine. As it was, it didn't even damage the crankshaft."

Her breath released in a rush. Finally, good news. For real this time.

Lately, she'd thought everything was looking up. After years waitressing in greasy spoons where tips were often in the form of coins rather than bills, she'd run into a girl she'd worked with years earlier. Rachel's recommendation had gotten her a job at La Maison D'Elise. It was one of those places with linen tablecloths, candlelight and live background music. And patrons who thought nothing of adding a forty- or fifty-dollar gratuity to their bill.

She'd even had a new boyfriend, someone with some class—someone who picked her up in a shiny, new Audi A5 convertible and took her places requiring attire other than holey jeans and a tank top.

He'd been a regular patron of La Maison, a successful photographer, with some high-profile modeling clients. She'd been so sure he was too good to be true, she'd turned him down for a solid three weeks before she'd finally agreed to go out with him.

Then, less than twenty-four hours ago, everything had blown up in her face. Now she had no boyfriend, no job and no home.

Alyssa had seen something she wasn't supposed to have seen and now some bad men wanted her dead. Her ex-boyfriend was one of them.

At least she still had a car and she hadn't

needed to wipe out her savings to get it fixed.

"Thank you. I appreciate you getting the work done so quickly."

"No problem. Jim said it was a rush job and put two of us on it."

She thanked him again and stepped back into the office as the man she'd seen earlier was hanging up the phone.

"Are you Jim?"

"I am."

"Alyssa Anderson, owner of the '92 Tempo."

"We've got you ready to go. That'll be two hundred dollars."

She took the pack from her back and removed ten twenty-dollar bills from her wallet. She had hit the ATM on her way out of town and pulled out five hundred dollars. Now her cash was almost half gone.

In the garage, one bay door and then the other rolled down on their tracks, the metallic rumble drifting into the office. The mechanic she'd spoken with earlier walked through the open door.

"'Night, boss." He gave Alyssa a salute. "Safe travels."

"Thanks."

She picked up her pack from the counter but didn't bother slipping her arms through the two straps. When she turned her attention back to Jim, he pulled a handwritten invoice from the top of one of the haphazard stacks on his desk. After writing "paid in full" across the bottom, he rose and handed it to her, along with her car key. "I'm right behind you."

He followed her out and locked the door then disappeared around the side of the building, probably headed to the Nissan she'd noticed earlier. The Trailblazer pulled from the parking lot, the mechanic at the wheel.

Alyssa glanced down at the invoice as she made her way toward her car. The top line of the description said, "Repairs to 1992 Ford Tempo." The list of what was involved was lengthy.

Far too lengthy for the two hundred dollars she'd been charged.

Her breath caught and her hands started to shake. The garage hadn't discounted the charges because they'd felt sorry for her. They knew nothing of her situation. No, the amount she owed was so low because someone else had paid the rest of the bill. Making sure the repair was affordable with her meager savings was the way to guarantee she would return. Otherwise, she would have abandoned the car and kept running.

She looked frantically around her at the empty parking lot. Nearby, the Nissan's engine roared to life. Then a car shot from the business catty-cornered, across the four lanes of traffic, barreling toward the Tempo.

Alyssa spun and retraced her steps at a full run, still clutching the loop on the top of the pack. She needed to reach Jim before he left.

As she rounded the corner of the building, the Nissan pulled onto the side road, headed away from her. Behind her, the car roared closer. Trees lined the property on the other side of the street. If she could make it across before the car hit her, she might have a chance at escape.

She shot into the road…right into the path of an SUV. The driver braked hard, the squeal of tires setting her teeth on edge.

As she glanced over her other shoulder, the car that had pursued her swerved toward the highway. Relief flooded her, but only for a moment. An arm extended through the open passenger window, and sunlight glinted off the barrel of a pistol.

Two shots rang out as she dove and rolled, tossing the pack. A searing pain stabbed through her left shoulder. She came to a stop in the narrow stretch of patchy grass lining the side of the street, the trees she had targeted only six feet away.

She sat up and grasped her shoulder with her other hand. The bullet had grazed her.

At least, she hoped that was all it was. The sleeve of her shirt was already wet. When she drew her hand away, her palm was covered with blood. Her wrist hurt, too. So did her knee. She'd probably injured them hitting the pavement.

When she tried to rise, pain shot through her right knee, sending her right back to the asphalt. *No, not this on top of everything else.* She looked frantically around. The car was gone.

The SUV had stopped—a later model white Land Rover. Its door swung open, and a sneaker-clad foot appeared beneath it. The driver likely wanted to make sure she wasn't hurt. She would tell him she was all right, thank him for stopping and send him on his way.

Alyssa pushed herself upright, hands splayed against the pavement, her weight on her left leg. After snatching up her pack, she again pressed her hand to her left shoulder. There was more blood than she'd initially thought. She'd deal with it later. Right now, she had more pressing things to concern herself with—like staying alive.

She limped toward the Good Samaritan, trying hard not to wince with each step, all the while casting frequent glances at the highway behind her. Still no sign of the car.

How had she even wound up in this situation? The scene had seemed so harmless: four businessmen sitting around a table discussing famous works of art. But what she'd witnessed had had more significance than she had initially thought. Maybe the art had been stolen. Or maybe the paintings they'd been talking about had been copies or fakes and they'd been marketing them as the real thing. The details didn't matter.

Because now some dangerous men were determined to keep her quiet.

She had to get out of there.

Spencer Cavanaugh slid from his Land Rover, heart pounding. Not only had a woman just run right into his path, he'd heard two pops. Maybe it had only been a vehicle backfiring, but with his windows up and radio on, it had sounded an awful lot like gunshots.

His hand shook as he reached for the back door handle. At his command, a chocolate Lab jumped from the back seat. He was still wearing his service dog vest from their trip to the U-Haul store to purchase more packing boxes.

The woman he had braked to avoid was staggering in his direction, clutching her left shoulder with the opposite hand. When she had run out in front of him, he hadn't observed her long enough to form an opinion of her condition. One moment, the road ahead of him had been clear. The next moment, she'd been darting into his path.

Now, the way she was stumbling, she looked injured. Her long, red hair hung in her face, twigs and leaves caught in the tangles. One leg of her jeans was ripped at the knee, and blood oozed between the fingers of the hand clutching her opposite shoulder. She cast frequent glances behind her, as if expecting an attack.

"Thanks for stopping." She came to a halt about three feet in front of him.

Apollo stood next to him, pressing his weight into the side of Spence's leg, just as he'd been trained to do in tense situations.

Without releasing her left shoulder, the woman raised that hand to fling her hair out of her face, turning toward the main highway as she did. "I'm all right. You don't need to stay."

His jaw went slack. In the final second before she'd turned, recognition had slammed into him.

Alyssa Ashbaugh? The red hair wasn't familiar. The face was—the green eyes, the full lips, the soft lines of her jaw. He'd long ago memorized every feature.

He removed his sunglasses. "You need a doctor."

"No, I'm fine. I have to get—" Her gaze

locked with his, and her eyes widened briefly before narrowing to slits.

Eight years earlier, he'd broken her heart. She obviously still hadn't forgiven him. But now wasn't the time to rehash the past.

"You're bleeding. Let me take you to the emergency room."

"It's just a nick. I don't need your help." Coldness underlay her tone. She spun to limp toward the mechanic shop next to them.

In two long strides, he'd reached her side, Apollo trotting next to him.

"Alyssa, don't be stubborn."

"I told you, I'm all right."

"You can hardly walk, and that's too much blood to classify as *all right*." Her sleeve was soaked with it and red rivulets trailed down her arm. His jaw dropped a second time. "You've been shot."

Those pops he'd heard hadn't been from a car backfiring. They'd been gunshots, one of which had found its mark.

She shrugged. "I'm sure it's just a flesh wound."

"Regardless, if someone is out there shooting at people, we need to call the police."

He pulled his phone from his pocket to dial 911. She continued her trek across the parking lot without acknowledging what he'd said. It was empty except for an older compact car that looked as if it had seen better days. Its body boasted at least three colors of paint, one of which was probably primer.

He grasped her right shoulder. She was still using that arm to stem the bleeding on the left. "Hold on, Alyssa. Where are you going?"

She shook off his hand. "See the old Ford Tempo up there? It's mine. I'm going to get in it and leave."

"What about your knee?"

"I'm more worried right now about getting gone before those guys come back."

"That's why we need to call the police."

He'd wondered if it had been a random drive-by shooting. Her statement told him it hadn't. Those guys had been gunning for her and apparently weren't going to give up.

She stared at him, features set in determination. "Calling the police isn't going to keep me alive."

"You can give them a description of the car. Maybe they can catch the guys."

"Gold sedan. That's all I know. I was too busy dodging bullets to zero in on things like the make and model of the car."

She turned away from him and limped a few more steps, obviously in pain.

He walked next to her. "You think the bleeding is going to stop on its own?"

"Eventually."

"And you're planning to drive with that knee."

"Yep."

"How do you think you'll do mashing the brake?"

She winced at the thought. "It'll be fine, or I'll use my left."

"You're sure your knee will be fine without care, enough to risk permanent damage?"

She hesitated, lips pressed together. Maybe he was getting through to her.

"And I'm guessing that, whoever these guys are, they know what you drive. You don't think they'll be watching for your car?"

Her steps slowed even more.

"Let me take you to the emergency room. The police can meet us there. The doctors will stitch up your shoulder and make sure there isn't a bullet lodged in there, and figure out what needs to be done for your knee."

After another moment of hesitation, she nodded. "Okay."

"Wait in your car while I bring my SUV over." He didn't want her to have to retrace her steps all the way back to the side road, but leaving her standing outside wasn't a good option, either.

"Okay."

He turned to hurry back to his truck, trying to disguise his own limp. With all the time he'd spent on his feet today, he wasn't quite successful. Twenty-six years old, and he sometimes walked like an old man.

He glanced over his shoulder, hoping Alyssa wouldn't take off before he could get back. He'd just have to trust her. Confiscating her key would have only ticked her off.

When he pulled into the space to her left a minute later, she was watching him through the side window. After swinging open the door, she slid from her car into his SUV, dragging the backpack with her.

The smile she flashed him held resignation. "Thanks."

"You're welcome." He handed her his phone.

"What's this for?"

"Since Georgia is a hands-free state, and sitting in the parking lot while I make the call wouldn't be the smartest move, I figured you could handle the 911 call while I drive."

When she hesitated, he continued. "Tell the dispatcher what you know and that we're on our way to the emergency room."

While she placed the call, he drove. When she identified herself as Alyssa Anderson, he did a double take. She was married? He glanced at her left hand. She wasn't wearing a ring. That didn't necessarily mean anything, though.

He continued to listen to the one-sided conversation. She couldn't describe the car, other than saying it was a gold sedan, and she had no information about either of the men inside, except that the passenger had a gun.

When she finished the call, she set his phone in the cup holder. "They're going to send an officer to the hospital to do a report, but I won't be able to tell him any more than I just told the dispatcher."

"Any idea who the men were?" Not that he really expected her to tell him.

"Not a clue."

"Do you live in LaGrange?" He'd been there a year and hadn't run into her. But in a town with a population of more than thirty thousand, that didn't mean much.

"No, Atlanta. I was just passing through when my car broke down."

"When did you move to Atlanta?"

"The first time? A year after you left. Then I lived in South Carolina, Alabama, Tennessee and a couple of other towns in Georgia before winding back up in Atlanta."

"That's a lot of moving around in seven years."

"I thought you were somewhere on the other side of the world, trying to be a hero."

He smiled at her description. That hadn't been his goal. At least, not at first. In fact, when he'd joined the army, it had been more for his own benefit than any sense of duty to his country. With all of the stupid decisions he'd made as a teenager, he'd been smart enough to recognize he'd needed to make some drastic changes. The discipline of the military had been the quickest way to that end.

"I'm not sure I can claim the hero title, but, yeah, I was on the other side of the world until a year ago. I did two tours in Afghanistan and then finished in Kuwait."

He'd reenlisted but only made it a few months before having to take a medical discharge. One of his buddies had lost a leg stepping on an IED, and another had lost his life taking an RPG to the gut. Yet, in spite of being in numerous combat situations himself, he'd managed to leave Afghanistan unscathed. Physically, anyway.

Then, after being in Kuwait a while, he'd swerved to miss hitting a kid, rolled the Jeep and shattered his hip. Two surgeries later, he'd been left with some serious metal and a limp he could hide pretty well unless he was really fatigued.

Alyssa nodded. "Now you're back. What made you choose LaGrange?"

"One of the guys I served with was from there."

He'd made a promise. After the grenade had done its damage, his buddy had held on just long enough to ask Spence to look after his wife until he knew she was going to be all right. That was exactly what he'd done. He'd fulfilled his obligation. His friend's widow had even agreed it was time for him to get on with his own life.

Now he was ready to move back to his hometown of Pensacola, Florida. He'd planned to spend the next two days packing. Putting off the move wasn't an option. The lease on his apartment was up in two days. Everything was set in Florida, too. He'd visited Alyssa's sisters a month ago and signed a lease for the other half of the Ashbaugh Charters building. It would house his living quarters as well as the retail space beneath. He was finally going to realize his dream of owning his own music store.

As he pulled into the emergency room parking lot, he retrieved his phone from the cup holder. "I'm going to drop you off at the door and then park."

"Are you coming in with me?"

"I was planning to."

"What about your dog?"

"He can come in with us." With his vest on, he was welcome anywhere Spence went. In fact, he hadn't been separated from Apollo since K9s For Warriors had hooked them up three months ago.

She nodded. "I'd like to get a dog some-day. My life just isn't very conducive to caring for an animal right now."

Yeah, it probably wasn't. He eased to a stop at the covered entrance. "We'll be in as soon as I park."

When he and Apollo walked through the automatic doors a few minutes later, Alyssa was still sitting in the waiting room. He took a seat in the chair to her left, and Apollo lay on the floor between their feet.

"They've checked you in?"

"Yes. She said they'll be calling me back in a few minutes."

He looked down at her shoulder and frowned. She was doing a good enough job of keeping pressure on the shoulder that she wouldn't bleed to death, but the injury had to be painful. Riding in an ambulance would have gotten her into triage a lot more quickly. At least the place wasn't packed. In fact, there were only two other people in the waiting room.

The automatic door slid open, and a LaGrange police officer stepped into the waiting area. His gaze scanned the room until it settled on Alyssa.

"Alyssa Anderson?"

"Yes."

"You reported a drive-by shooting." He took a chair on her other side. "What can you tell me?"

"I was at Jim's Garage, picking up my car. When I came outside, there was a car waiting in the convenience store parking lot catty-cornered from there. I didn't notice it until it shot out of the parking lot and crossed the street, headed right for me. I ran across the side street there, right out in front of him." On *him*, she tilted her head toward Spence. "That's when they fired the shots."

As she talked, the officer jotted notes in his pad. Finally, he looked at her. "Did you recognize the car these people were in?"

"No."

"Can you describe it?"

"It was a four-door, gold, not new but not old, either. I'm not even sure what kind. There wasn't anything that stood out about it, but I was more focused on trying to stay alive at that point."

"Any idea who the shooter was, or why he was aiming at you?"

She shook her head but didn't meet the officer's gaze. "No clue."

Spence studied her. She was lying. At least, she knew more than she was letting on.

After a few more questions, which Alyssa was unable—or unwilling—to answer, a nurse called her back.

The officer stood. "I've got your phone number. If I need anything else, I'll call you."

Spence stood, too. Alyssa didn't object, so he followed her. Apollo walked right next to him, ever alert. The Lab's demeanor always went from relaxed to "on duty" the moment Spence picked up the service dog vest, and it stayed that way until he removed it.

The nurse led them into one of the triage areas and, after Alyssa took a seat on the bed, pulled the curtain around on its track. Spence eased into the nearby chair, and Apollo lay next to him. After she had taken Alyssa's history and her vitals, she left the area.

"How are you feeling?"

"All right. My shoulder's throbbing, but I'm pretty sure a shot is going to take care of that pretty soon. Then it'll get stitched up and be good as new." She put a hand on each side of her right knee and slowly straightened her leg. "I'm not sure about this, though. I'm hoping I haven't done serious damage."

"Me, too." Especially if she was running from someone. "Do you need to let anyone know what happened? Wouldn't *Mr.* Anderson want to know you're here?"

Her eyebrows drew together. "Who?" The confusion cleared. "No, I'm not married. Never have been. As soon as I left home, I ditched the Ashbaugh name. Haven't been back since."

Before he could respond, a doctor walked in and introduced himself. Another nurse wheeled in a rolling table.

The doctor picked up a syringe. "We're going to numb this and see what we've got. If it's just a graze like you suspect, a few stitches should do it."

Alyssa dropped her hand. "Sounds good."

Since Spence was sitting on her right, he couldn't see her injury or watch what the medical folks were doing to tend to her. After the doctor administered the injection, the nurse approached with a sterile cloth and wound cleaner.

So, Alyssa wasn't married. She had changed her name, likely to escape her past. He wasn't surprised. With an alcoholic father, a mother who'd taken off when Alyssa was fifteen, and two older sisters she'd never been close to, she didn't have a lot of fond memories of her family. Maybe he was part of the childhood she was trying to forget.

His chest tightened. He hadn't wanted to hurt her. He just hadn't had a choice.

At eighteen, he'd witnessed a best friend die from an overdose. By then, he had begun to develop his own drug habit. The experience had shaken him up enough to scare him clean. But at the time, Alyssa hadn't been ready to give up anything.

Neither had his other friends. Staying in the town where he'd grown up, hanging with the people he'd hung with his entire childhood, the pull of his old life had been too strong.

So he'd walked away from everything— his friends, his dysfunctional family and the only girl he'd ever truly loved—and joined the army. That decision had probably saved his life. The irony still struck him—the thought he'd been more likely to survive Afghanistan than Pensacola.

But that wasn't the only irony. It was while he'd belonged to the US government and his life was not his own that he'd discovered true freedom. During his first tour in Afghanistan, while pinned down by enemy fire, he'd promised God if He would spare his life, he'd give Him whatever time he had left.

God had, and Spence had kept his side of the bargain. He was still keeping it.

Alyssa really needed what he'd found. From what he had observed during their brief encounter this afternoon, she hadn't changed much. The toughness she'd always had was still there. So was the chip on her shoulder.

Regardless of what she had said to the cop about not knowing who had shot at her, something told him she wasn't simply an innocent victim. She'd seriously ticked someone off—enough to try to kill her. Maybe she had outgrown her propensity to find trouble, but it had obviously found her.

As much as he wished otherwise, he wouldn't be in her life long enough to help her navigate her way out of whatever mess she was in. Wherever she was headed, it wouldn't be Pensacola. She obviously wanted nothing to do with her childhood home.

He would stay with her this evening. The doctor was currently stitching her shoulder. Then they would have to do X-rays and possibly an MRI on her knee. But once Alyssa was finished at the emergency room, she would insist they go their separate ways. And he'd never see her again.

With the thought, a sense of heaviness pressed down on him—sadness and regret. But most of all, worry. What had she gotten involved with that had her fleeing for her life?

She needed to tell the police everything she knew. They couldn't go after the threat if she refused to talk. But unless she had changed a lot over the past eight years, that wasn't going to happen. When she had her mind made up, there was no changing it.

How could he protect her when she stubbornly refused help?

TWO

Moans and groans came from the other side of the drawn curtain.

Alyssa looked at Spence and heaved a sigh. They had watched the other patient come in thirty minutes ago, hunched over in a wheelchair, both arms wrapped around her abdomen. She had complained of stomach pain that had begun that morning and gotten more severe as the day had progressed.

Another moan came from a few feet away, rising in volume and ending on a wail. Alyssa rolled her eyes. She wasn't unsympathetic. She was just antsy. She really wanted to get out of there.

The ER doctor had already stitched up her shoulder. The bullet had made clear entry and exit wounds, with a bloody path between, so he was confident it wasn't lodged in the tissue. Now, one shot and eighteen stitches later, she was patched up, the bleeding stopped. The doctor had assured her it would heal fine, but to take it easy for a few days. Without knowing what the immediate future held, she couldn't guarantee how closely she'd be following that advice.

Now she was waiting for the results of an MRI of her knee. Although she hadn't wanted to spend the extra time there, she hadn't argued. She'd tried to put her full weight on the leg while transferring from the wheelchair to the bed when she'd first arrived. The pain that had shot through her knee had almost taken her breath away.

Spence was still sitting in the chair immediately to her right, her backpack leaning against its front leg, the dog lying next to him. Having Spence there had been all right. He hadn't plied her with questions, as she'd feared. Instead, he'd kept up a fairly steady stream of small talk, which was good. She'd seen his look of doubt when she'd told the officer she didn't know who had shot her. Spence obviously hadn't believed her.

But she'd told the truth. She really didn't know who'd been in the car. She hadn't felt the need to admit she'd known who'd ordered her execution. With no idea who she could trust, her best bet was to reveal as little information as possible.

He reached beside him to scratch the top of the Lab's head. "You mentioned you were en route from Atlanta when your car broke down but didn't say where you were headed."

"Pensacola."

At his raised brows, she frowned. "I was going back for my mom's graveside service. Since I've now missed it, those plans are scrapped."

His brow creased. "Your mom came back?"

"She never left."

"Wait a minute. I was there."

Yeah, he had been. They'd just struck up a friendship when her mom disappeared. She'd been fifteen, he'd been sixteen. It hadn't taken them long to move from just friends to boyfriend and girlfriend.

She drew in a deep breath. "Turns out my dad killed her, buried her and had the gazebo built over the site. His secret would have stayed buried forever if the last hurricane hadn't destroyed the gazebo."

"Whoa, that's some heavy stuff."

He raised his right arm to run his palm over the top and down the back of his head. Sometime in the past eight years, he'd spent time in the gym, evident in both his flexed arm and the way the T-shirt stretched taut across his chest. He'd always worn his dark-brown hair a little on the long side. Not anymore. It wasn't as severe as a military haircut, but it was nowhere near the length he'd had in his pre-army days. She couldn't say she didn't like it. It made him look capable, mature, one hundred percent masculine.

She tamped down the old attraction that had risen so unexpectedly and shrugged. "His killing her was an accident. At least, that's what he claimed."

"I'm sorry."

The Lab rose from his place on the floor beside Spence and approached the bed. Alyssa scratched him on the back of the neck, and he rested his head on her lap. For the past hour, the dog had alternated between lying next to Spence and rising to check on her.

While Spence's presence had been tolerable, Apollo's had been awesome. He acted as if he sensed her anxiety and wanted to offer her comfort. What kind of service did the dog provide for Spence? He'd apparently been injured. Although he seemed to try to walk as normally as possible, there was an awkwardness to his gait, a slight limp. Not wanting to pry, she hadn't asked. At one time, no topic would have been off limits. That had changed.

Another groan drifted through the closed curtain. Alyssa hoped the woman would get some relief soon, for all of their sakes.

Apollo moved away from the bed, but instead of lying next to the chair, he sat and put a paw on Spence's leg.

Spence looked from the dog to her. "I think he needs to go out. Will you be okay for a few minutes?"

"Of course. Bored maybe, but okay. Take your time. The poor boy has been cooped up for a while."

Shortly after Spence and Apollo walked out, footsteps approached and fell silent outside the curtain sectioning her space off from the rest of the room. Apollo and Spence couldn't be back already. They'd left just two minutes ago. Maybe the doctor was there, ready to give her the results of the MRI and send her home.

Fingers wrapped the edge of the curtain. A moment later, it lifted to the side.

A man stepped through, and the curtain fell back into place.

This wasn't the doctor, and it wasn't either of the radiology people she'd seen earlier. In fact, she hadn't had any previous contact with him.

"I'm here to give you something for pain."

What pain? Her shoulder was still numb from the injections they'd given her before stitching her up. Lying in bed, her knee wasn't even bothering her, other than a deep ache.

Alyssa swept the length of him with her gaze. Instead of those cotton-type pants nurses often wore, he was dressed in blue jeans, tennis shoes covering his feet. If he had a name badge, it was hidden beneath his zipped jacket. So was whatever uniform top he might be wearing. The jacket was also hiding a lot of bulk, which she guessed was ninety-five percent muscle.

She shook her head. "That's okay. I don't need anything."

He gave her a slight smile. Maybe it was supposed to be reassuring, but it fell short of reaching his eyes.

"The doctor disagrees. He wants you to have this before you leave." He slipped a hand into his jacket pocket and pulled out a syringe.

What kind of nurse carries a syringe in their pocket? She scooted away from him on the narrow bed, her pulse kicking into high gear. She'd always considered herself street smart. Maybe she was paranoid, too. Because something about this man set off every internal alarm she had.

He stepped closer. "Relax. It'll just be a little prick."

"No." She pushed herself into a seated position, her tone emphatic. "I said I don't want anything. You need to leave."

Indecision settled across his features. But it didn't last long. He moved the syringe to his left hand and curled his right into a fist. A split second later, that fist flew toward her face.

Alyssa twisted and threw herself over the side rail of the bed and then hit the floor with a thud. She released a scream, loud and long, and scrambled to her feet. The curtain between her bed and the next slid back, and the woman who had the stomach issues stood there, slightly hunched, mouth agape, alarm in her eyes, her own pain apparently forgotten.

The man with the syringe looked from Alyssa to the woman and back to Alyssa again before darting from the room. There was a clatter in the hall, followed by shouts.

Alyssa looked frantically around, searching for anything she might use to protect herself if he came back. He'd been determined to give her whatever was in the syringe. Since she wouldn't take it willingly, he'd tried to knock her out so he could administer it while she was unconscious.

The sound of approaching footsteps sent panic through her again, and she fell into a fighting stance, fists raised. It was only one of the nurses.

"Are you all right?"

Alyssa lowered herself to the bed, panting, her legs suddenly weak. Now that some of the adrenaline was starting to dissipate, her knee was screaming. She put a hand on each side of her kneecap and gently massaged the swollen joint.

She looked back up at the nurse. "The man who just ran out of here, wearing the jeans and jacket, he wasn't one of your people, was he?"

"No, he wasn't. After knocking a couple of us down in the hallway, he escaped out the emergency room entrance. We've called hospital security. I'm sure they'll want to talk to you."

Yeah, they probably would. But there wasn't much she could tell them. She didn't know who he was or what was in the syringe. But one thing was sure. If he'd been successful in giving her that injection, she'd have left the ER in a body bag.

Spence stepped up next to the nurse, Apollo's leash in one hand. "Is everything all right?" His gaze shifted from Alyssa to the nurse and back again. "The hallway seems to be in a bit of an uproar."

Alyssa pressed her lips into a thin line. "Somebody insisted on giving me an injection I didn't want."

Spence frowned. "What kind of injection?"

"A lethal one, I'm guessing. The guy who shot me apparently decided to finish what he'd started."

His eyes widened. "Apollo and I were heading back when I saw someone run from the building. I'm sure it was the same guy. The doors hadn't even finished opening when he slipped between them and took off. I should have pursued him."

"And both you and Apollo could have been shot." Spence needed to stay out of her business. She had enough problems without having to worry about him going all Rambo on her and getting himself killed.

Before either of them could argue the point further, the security guard stepped into the space. The nurse walked away, leaving the three of them and the dog alone.

The man introduced himself as Tom Atkins and asked the same type of questions the police officer had asked. Alyssa's answers remained the same, too. She couldn't tell them what she didn't know.

And she didn't feel safe telling them what she did.

Throughout the conversation, Spence looked on her with disapproval. From his position in her peripheral vision, that judgment was something she felt rather than saw. But it was there.

Fine, let him judge. Soon she would be out of there—away from LaGrange and away from Spence and the judgment and disappointment in his eyes.

As Atkins was finishing his report, the doctor walked in. He was wearing a smile.

"I have good news. Your anterior and posterior cruciate ligaments look good, no tears that we can see. Same for the meniscus. No fractures, either. Looks like you just have a bad sprain. Take it easy for a few days. Ice the knee for twenty minutes every two or three hours. We'll send you home with an elastic knee brace. If you've got a set of crutches, that might help, too."

"Thank you."

Relief collided with dread. They were sending her home. The address she'd given them on the paperwork was where she'd lived for the past eight months. But it wasn't home. Not anymore.

Besides having nowhere to go, she wasn't even sure she could make it back to her car. She could call a cab, but what if the men who wanted her dead were hiding out in the hospital parking lot or waiting for her at Jim's Garage?

She would call the police. Surely, after

two attempts on her life, she would be able to get a unit to follow the cab from the hospital to the garage and make sure she got away safely.

At least she wouldn't have to handle the financial end of things on her way out. Someone had brought the paperwork to the triage room shortly after she'd arrived, and she'd proudly provided her insurance card. That great job she'd landed had actually come with health benefits.

When the doctor left, Alyssa finally made eye contact with Spence. His jaw was tight, his eyebrows drawn together. Yep, just what she'd suspected. He was judging her.

He frowned. "You told both the police and the security guard that you have no idea who's after you."

"That's because I *don't* know."

He leaned forward in his chair and studied her some more, so intently she could hardly keep from fidgeting.

"What's going on, Alyssa? What did you

do?" He released a sigh heavy with disappointment. That same disappointment was reflected in his eyes.

She hadn't set out to be a disappointment to everyone she cared about, but that seemed to be her lot in life.

She crossed her arms and glared at him. "I didn't do anything."

"So, a random drive-by shooter followed you all the way to the hospital to finish you off. And you have no idea why he's after you."

A nurse walked in with the brace the doctor had promised, sparing Alyssa from having to respond to Spence's accusations. She slipped one foot through and pulled the brace into place over the top of her jeans. No way would it fit underneath.

"What are you going to do now?"

She carefully slid her right foot into her tennis shoe without looking at him. "I'm going to call a cab."

Spence would insist on driving her back to the garage, but this was her battle, not his. If these men decided to take pot shots at her, she didn't want him anywhere in the vicinity. She started to tie the laces and then hesitated. She wouldn't put Spence in danger, but what about the cab driver, possibly a man with a wife and kids? Even with the police following, someone could still be hurt.

Spence heaved a sigh that sounded a lot like one a parent might expel when dealing with a difficult child. It sent a shot of annoyance through her.

The same quality she'd heard in his sigh came through in his tone. "So you're going to walk out of here with no plan and no way to defend yourself."

She finished lacing her shoes and straightened. "And I suppose *you* have that plan."

If he did, she was willing to hear it. Because she was no longer feeling as confident as she had when she'd come in.

"Actually, I do. How's this? I call a friend of mine to meet us here. He radios Dispatch to send some of his law enforcement buddies. They make sure we get from here to the garage and see you safely out of town."

Wow. Someone with connections. Definitely a better plan than hers.

"Where are you going after you leave here? Something tells me you're not going back to Atlanta."

"I don't know."

"You don't know, or you won't tell me? Come on, Alyssa. Regardless of who these guys are and why they're after you, you've got to be willing to accept some help."

A stony hardness wrapped around her heart. "I don't need you to take care of me." She didn't try to soften the flinty tone. "Eight years ago, maybe. But you took off."

He winced and pain filled his eyes.

Guilt pricked her. She half understood why he'd done what he had, but that didn't make it any easier.

He sighed again, but this one held resignation. "You've had two attempts on your life in a span of less than four hours. Do you think these men are going to just give up and leave you alone?"

She drew her lower lip between her teeth. No, they probably wouldn't.

When she didn't respond, he continued. "I was planning to leave for Pensacola the day after tomorrow, but I can go earlier. Come back with me."

He had to be joking. "There's nothing for me there."

"You have family. Two sisters whose fiancés happen to be cops."

What? He'd stayed in touch with Kassie and Kris and neither of them had bothered to mention it?

Alyssa closed her eyes, tamping down the swirling emotions and forcing herself to look at everything logically. She'd lashed out when he'd said it, but Spence was right. If she hoped to get out of the mess she was in, she would have to accept some help.

It wasn't easy. She'd taken care of herself since she'd left home at eighteen. Actually, she'd taken care of herself before then. She'd lost her mother at fifteen. In the years that had followed, her father had climbed out of the bottle just long enough to rake her over the coals for her infractions. Two years after losing her mother, Spence had left. She'd made it one more year, finishing high school before taking off herself.

Now, at twenty-five, having to rely on anybody rankled. Having to rely on Spence really stuck in her craw. And having to crawl to her sisters was almost unthinkable. They'd always judged her. Now that they were both regular churchgoers, they probably thought that gave them an even better platform from which to look down on her. She didn't need them or their faith.

But as much as she didn't want to admit it, accepting help, even if it came from Spence or her sisters, beat the alternative. Because this time, she really *was* in over her head. After walking in on that conversation, she had slipped right back out, but not before the men had noticed. Her boyfriend had promised the other three he would take care of it. She'd managed to escape before he'd had the opportunity.

Since then, Peter and his cronies had come after her twice. They would keep coming until they succeeded. They wouldn't give up until she was dead.

Weapons, lethal injections, thugs to do their bidding—these men apparently had unlimited resources to make that happen.

Spence stood just to the side of the emergency room's automatic glass doors, peering out into the night. Apollo stood next to him, ever alert. Alyssa had walked from the treatment area and, after stopping by the restroom to change out of her bloody shirt, had taken a seat in one of the waiting room chairs.

When she had stood from the bed, he'd offered her his arm. She'd passed, claiming she was going to have to be able to walk on her own. After gingerly putting her weight on her right leg, she'd taken a step and then another. She wouldn't be running any races, but the brace helped. She was at least able to walk.

It had taken a lot of convincing, but he'd finally gotten her to agree to go to Pensacola and let him follow her. He wished he could stay there with her rather than having to immediately head back to La-Grange.

The only other option would have been to keep her with him until he could clear out his apartment and head south for good. Knowing there were men who wanted her dead hiding nearby, that would have been a bad plan. The sooner he could get her away from LaGrange, the safer she would be.

So, he was following her out tonight and leaving her in the care of her sisters first thing tomorrow morning. He wasn't sure about Kassie's housing, but Kris still lived in the family home on Bayou Texar. The place was huge. Hopefully, it would be large enough for the two sisters to share without coming to blows. When they'd all been teenagers, it hadn't been because the animosity between them had been so great. From his brief contact with Alyssa this afternoon, it didn't sound like those relationships had improved much.

Headlights drew closer, and a vehicle stopped under the porte cochere. He motioned to Alyssa. "Here's our ride. To my truck anyway."

Jason wasn't just one of his best friends. He was also a detective with the LaGrange Police Department. He was in his personal vehicle, but he'd assured Spence there would be others, some marked, some unmarked, who would follow them from the hospital to Spence's apartment to Jim's Garage, and well out of town, all the way to the Georgia/Alabama line.

Alyssa rose from the chair she'd been sitting in and limped to the door, which slid back on its track. Spence handed Alyssa the leash and held up a hand. As he stepped out, he looked around. There was activity—two vehicles that appeared to be heading toward the exit, another sliding into a parking spot. No gold sedans. That didn't mean anything. The men could have swapped vehicles.

He opened the front passenger door of Jason's Kia Soul. "Thanks, buddy. I appreciate this."

"Don't mention it."

Spence motioned at Alyssa, and she stepped outside, Apollo next to her. After passing off the leash, she tossed her backpack on the floorboard then sat and swung both legs inside. Once he and Apollo had climbed into the back seat, Jason pulled away from the entrance. Spence made brief introductions and directed him to where he had parked.

Jason eased to a stop behind the Land Rover. "There are a couple of unmarked units here in the parking lot and another at your place. A third is circling the area around Jim's Garage." He glanced over at

Alyssa. "Whoever these guys are, we're hoping to get them off the street before you even get away from LaGrange."

Alyssa nodded. "Thank you."

Her gratitude seemed genuine, in spite of the fact that getting her to this point had involved a battle. She swung open her door. As Spence stepped out, she twisted in her seat, preparing to exit herself. When she tossed her hair over her right shoulder, some of the wavy red locks trailed across the side of the bucket seat.

Her natural hair color was a medium brown. Over the years, he'd seen it jet-black and several shades of blond. The red looked good on her.

She looked good. All three of the Ashbaugh girls were short—no more than five foot three or four. But where twins Kassie and Kris had always had sleek, athletic builds, Alyssa had always been curvier. Even their facial features were different, which had led to claims by Alyssa's father that she wasn't his, claims their mother denied.

After once again thanking his friend, Spence walked Alyssa to the passenger door of his Land Rover and instructed Apollo to hop into the back seat. As he turned onto Medical Drive, headed away from the hospital, Alyssa twisted to look at the dog. His tail immediately began to thud against the leather.

Spence stopped at a traffic light. She had twisted a little further but still couldn't reach the back seat. Apollo accommodated her by stepping forward and resting his head on the center console.

"You're a sweet boy." Alyssa scratched his neck and then worked her way down his back as far as she could reach.

Behind him, Apollo's tail continued to thud against the seat. The light changed, and Spence stepped on the accelerator. When he slid Alyssa a sideways glance, she was smiling. It hadn't taken him long to notice that the stiffness she displayed with him disappeared when she interacted with his dog, who now stood with his front legs on the floor, his back haunches still on the rear seat. The position didn't look comfortable. But Apollo seemed to have a knack for recognizing who needed his calming presence.

She looked at Spence. "He's a Lab, right?"

"He is."

"Labs are good dogs."

He nodded. Apollo was the best.

"How long have you had him?"

"Three months." During that time, the dog had brought him out of numerous nightmares and even staved off a few flash-backs. But he'd done so much more. He'd given Spence a new lease on life.

During those months he had waited to be matched with a dog, he'd found him-self withdrawing from life. Going out in public had become increasingly more dif-ficult. Soon he'd been ordering grocer-ies and anything else he'd needed online, stepping outside only to bring in packages and walk to the mailbox. Getting Apollo had brought him back into society.

As Alyssa continued to pet and coo at his dog, a heaviness settled in Spence's chest. He'd really hoped by now her life would be on track. She had always had a good heart, had never wanted to hurt anybody. She just hadn't been wise in her choice of friends…or firm in fighting bad influences. Regrettably, *he'd* been one of those bad influences back in the day.

He released a sigh. Whatever she was tangled up in, maybe she would share with him eventually. She used to tell him everything. That sharing had gone both ways.

They'd had a lot in common, the least of which had been alcoholic fathers. While his had tried to whip him into submission with fists, belts or whatever he could put his hands on, hers had simply beat her down with words. Or ignored her altogether. And they'd both dealt with the fallout in the most destructive ways possible.

Spence pulled into the parking lot of his

apartment complex and eased to a stop in one of the spaces. Jason's Soul appeared briefly in his rearview mirror as it passed behind him. The other vehicle that had exited the hospital parking lot behind Jason's had pulled in also, selecting a spot two spaces before reaching the Land Rover.

He swung open the door and stepped out. "I'm going to grab a change of clothes and some dog food. Will you be all right staying out here with Apollo?"

"I'll be fine, especially with Jason and the other guys keeping an eye on me."

He nodded. He wouldn't leave her otherwise. He would have made her hobble up with him. He'd have even carried her if he'd had to.

A few minutes later, he headed back down the stairs carrying a duffel bag filled with some toiletries, one change of clothes, two cans of Blue Buffalo and Apollo's food and water bowl. While in his apartment, he'd slid his Glock into the end pocket of the bag. He hadn't been armed today but he would be from here on out. At least until the men after Alyssa had been captured and locked up.

When he reached the parking lot, Jason was standing at the open passenger door of the Land Rover, talking to Alyssa. Spence slung the bag onto the floorboard behind the driver's seat and removed the pistol. It would ride in the center console.

Jason patted the roof twice. "I'll follow you to the garage. Two or three others will be there, too. They'll escort you all the way to the state line."

Alyssa gave him a grateful smile. "I don't know if this escort service is standard or if I'm getting special treatment because of you and Spence, but please let everyone know I'm really grateful."

Jason tilted his head. "Glad to be of service."

When they arrived at Jim's Garage ten minutes later, her car waited in the soft glow of one of the parking lot lights. Whatever had been wrong with it, he hoped the garage had fixed the problem and no new ones would crop up before they reached Pensacola.

He stopped next to the old car as Jason turned around some distance away, ready to pull back out onto the highway.

Alyssa gave Apollo a couple more scratches on the head. "Thank you."

"I'll be right behind you. I'm not telling you to drive crazy, but the sooner we can get you to Pensacola, the better I'll feel."

"I agree."

She climbed from the Land Rover, dragging her pack with her. As she tossed it into the back of the Tempo and slid into the driver's seat, he glanced around. Jason was still sitting where he had parked. Spence didn't see the others, but according to his friend, they were there. He pulled his phone from his pocket and sent Jason a quick text.

Thanks again. I'll let you know when we arrive.

Alyssa's door closed and he dropped his phone into the cup holder with a relieved sigh. She was safe for the time being. No one would be able to get to her.

But what if while one guy had been at the hospital trying to administer a lethal injection, another had been carrying out a contingency plan and planting a bomb on her car? Cold dread washed through him. He swung open his door and laid on the horn. Alyssa looked over at him, and he jumped from the SUV. Her face was in shadow, but he could guess what was there—alarm.

He hadn't wanted to startle her, but someone needed to thoroughly check her car before she cranked it, even if it delayed their leaving.

As he moved toward her, a low rumble rose above the hum of the Land Rover's engine. Her car was already running. She had apparently started it the same time he'd blown his horn. And it was all in one piece. He heaved a sigh of relief, gave her an okay sign and got back into his vehicle.

When she pulled from the parking lot, he was right behind her. Less than a block away, they passed a dark SUV sitting at the edge of a convenience store parking lot. It pulled out but stayed several car lengths back.

For the next twenty miles, they would be under the watchful eye of the LaGrange Police Department. Then they would cross the line into Alabama, and it would be up to him.

He had no idea what Alyssa had gotten involved in. But it didn't matter. He would still do everything in his power to protect her. She wasn't his responsibility. She certainly wasn't his girlfriend, because she wasn't even his friend. But he couldn't turn his back on her.

Maybe he was trying to make up for the past. Maybe, after serving his country for the majority of his adult life, the need to protect was ingrained in him.

Or maybe she had never totally vacated that special place in his heart.

After several turns, they merged onto Interstate 85. It didn't take Alyssa long to accelerate to the seventy-mile-an-hour speed limit. The gap between her and a semi in front of her narrowed, and she moved into the left lane. Two more times, she went around slower traffic and returned to the right lane.

Ahead, a sign welcomed them to Alabama. When he glanced in his rearview mirror, the SUV he'd observed earlier decelerated and made a U-turn in an emergency break in the median.

He glanced at the clock on the dashboard. The time was nearing ten. The sky was dark. If the moon was up there, it was hidden by clouds.

Over the next hour, traffic grew increasingly sparse. Headlights approached from behind, rapidly gaining on him. He cast frequent glances in his rearview mirror, waiting for the left turn signal to come on. Was the person behind him a reckless, aggressive driver who was going to wait until the last minute to go around him? Or had Alyssa's enemies found her again?

As the vehicle drew closer, a little of the tension seeped from his shoulders. Those were pickup truck headlights. They were too high to belong to the car Alyssa had described.

The driver did wait until the last minute to change lanes. But instead of continuing past him, he decelerated suddenly to travel next to him.

It was definitely a pickup—a large one, like an F-250 or a Silverado 2500. He jammed on his brakes, sending Apollo crashing into the back of his seat. At the same moment, the truck swerved into his lane. Its right rear bumper caught his left front one, and his back end swung around. Spence overcorrected, sending the vehicle hurtling toward oncoming traffic. For several seconds, his SUV followed a wild zigzag path, headed for the median one second and the tree-lined edge of the road the next. He fought to regain control, his heart pounding in his throat. *God help us!*

The wheel jerked in his hand as the Land Rover left the highway. He bounced over the uneven terrain, praying he wouldn't roll the vehicle and Apollo would come through unhurt. His foot on the brake did nothing to slow his forward momentum. He hit a ditch, and the wheel jerked right then left then right again.

His head snapped sideways, slamming into the side window, and the sharp sound of cracking glass filled the vehicle. Trees loomed large through the front windshield. The crash of metal and the explosion of the airbag happened simultaneously.

His ears rang, an annoying sound that grew louder as darkness closed in from all around.

Then there was nothing.

THREE

Alyssa sped down the road, maintaining a death grip on the steering wheel, a sob rising in her throat. A vehicle had just run Spence off the road. It had to be a truck, a rather large one. Its headlights were quite a bit higher than Spence's.

At the speed they were going, once the Land Rover left the road, it hadn't stood a chance. The uneven ground between the shoulder and tree line several yards away had tossed the SUV around like a toy, headlights making erratic paths through the darkness.

She hit her brakes. As she watched in her rearview mirror, the SUV came to an abrupt stop, lights shining diagonally across the road. Had Spence slammed into a tree?

Now the truck was gaining on her. Of course. They had only attacked Spence because he was with her. Anyone watching them would have guessed they were traveling together. Spence had maintained a distance of about five or six car lengths behind her, and every time she changed lanes, he had, too.

She stepped hard on the gas. Trying to outrun the truck was pointless. The gap closed and it moved into the left lane. Soon it was beside her.

Panic pounded up her spine. There was no one to help her. The driver of the truck had waited until she and Spence were in a gap in traffic. Although several sets of oncoming headlights were close, the traffic behind her was too far away for anyone to even recognize her distress. In front of her, taillights were visible far in the distance.

She glanced over in time to see the truck's passenger window lower. An arm extended through the open window. Without waiting to see what he held, she jerked the wheel to the left and slammed into the truck. The ear-splitting pop of a gunshot accompanied the sharp crunch of metal against metal.

The impact ricocheted her car in the other direction, sending her off the right shoulder. She jammed on the brakes and jerked the wheel back to the left. The truck was ahead of her now, and she was racing toward the center median. A few yards away, headlights moved rapidly in her direction.

A quarter turn of the wheel in the opposite direction sent her back off the right shoulder and bouncing along the uneven ground. Trees sped past, illuminated in the beams of her headlights. Her steering wheel turned sharply side to side, as if controlled by someone else.

Suddenly, a huge pine stood right in front of her, not twenty feet away. She made a hard left just in time to avoid hitting it head on, but not in time to miss it altogether.

The Tempo shuddered as the tree scraped along its side from front quarter panel to rear bumper. At the sudden abrupt stop, her head snapped forward, her face barely missing the steering wheel. There was no airbag. Her car had been made several years before they'd become mandatory.

She sat for several moments, panting, hands still gripping the wheel. Her head and neck hurt, and her skull seemed to be stuffed with cotton. Looking behind her in the side mirror, she could no longer see the Land Rover's headlights. Maybe she had travelled farther than she'd thought.

When she looked ahead, the truck had pulled off the road. Its backup lights brightened as it began to move toward her. They were coming back for her. If she sat there trying to collect her wits, she would end up dead.

The truck slowed and the passenger door swung open. She jumped from her car and ran around its rear and toward the woods, ignoring the pain stabbing through her knee. As she disappeared into the tree line, two shots rang out. One pinged off a tree just ahead and less than two feet to her right. A spray of bark hit her in the face.

A cold male voice reached her over the rustle of the branches that slapped her as she passed. "I'll take care of her. You make sure whoever was following her isn't going to give us any grief."

Her knees almost buckled, and her stomach dropped like a boulder. They were going after Spence. He was armed—he'd told her he would be. But was he in any shape to use what he was carrying? Was he even conscious? She had to do something.

Up ahead and to her left, something large suddenly crashed through the underbrush. She leaped sideways, away from whatever creature she had startled.

Several shots rang out in rapid succession, and she stifled a shriek. Hand pressed over her mouth, she ducked behind a large tree, molding herself against its bark.

There was more movement, this time behind her. She held her breath as her assailant passed within ten or fifteen feet of where she stood. He was moving at a jog, pistol drawn.

Alyssa slunk around the tree, keeping it between herself and the man who was hunting her. Suddenly, the footsteps stopped, and she peered out from her hiding place. He was looking slowly side to side, weapon apparently following his gaze.

She closed her eyes, afraid to even breathe. *Keep going.* If he continued to follow whatever they had heard, she could double back. Maybe she could get to Spence.

And do what? She wasn't even armed. If he was incapacitated, she would be powerless to help him.

A vise clamped down on her chest. She

should never have agreed to allow him to follow her. She should have given him a flat-out no and finagled a way out of the mess she was in without involving him. She'd tried. She should have tried harder. Instead, she had pulled him into her drama. Now he might pay with his life.

There was a rustle deeper in the woods, probably a deer or whatever she had heard earlier.

The man headed off in that direction.

She waited until she could no longer hear his footsteps. If she couldn't hear him, he likely couldn't hear her. Then she turned to retrace her steps. Maybe she could make it back to the interstate and try to flag someone down. Or better yet, get to her phone and call for help.

Alyssa crept forward as quietly as she could, the traffic ahead helping to mask her steps. Finally, she reached the edge of the trees and hesitated. She wouldn't step from their cover until she made sure no one was waiting beside her car.

Of course, they weren't. One of the men was pretty deep in the woods by now. The other had hiked back to the wrecked Land Rover. With his military training, Spence would be a formidable foe.

Unless he was unconscious.

But she hadn't yet heard a gunshot. That had to be a good sign.

The rumble of a semitruck grew louder, and she stepped from the line of trees. No one was standing next to her car or anywhere in its vicinity. She moved closer. So did the semi, the glow of the headlight beams spilling off the shoulder and barely reaching the edge of her car.

She stifled a gasp and froze.

Someone was sitting in her back seat, looking down at something in his lap. Was he going through her things? Looking for a way to get to her through something on her phone?

He would be out of luck there. Since it was a burner phone, she hadn't saved any contacts, had no social media accounts to link, hadn't sent or received any calls except the one from Jim's Garage.

So how many men were pursuing her?

At least three.

Without taking her eyes from the car, she crept backward, slipping silently into the woods.

If it was two against three, she and Spence weren't badly outnumbered.

But with one weapon between them, they were far outgunned.

Spence peered around a large pine tree, his pistol in his right hand, Apollo pressed against his left leg. Five minutes ago, he'd been oblivious to everything around him. He'd awoken to moans of pain. It had taken him several seconds to realize those moans were his own.

The next thing that had registered was a series of soft whimpers and a wet tongue slurping up his cheek. Through the cracked front windshield, a narrow beam of light some distance ahead had swung toward him then toward the ground, up and down. With the brain fog starting to clear, it hadn't taken him long to realize someone carrying a flashlight was walking in his direction.

He hadn't known whether it was a passerby who had noticed his SUV, pulled over and come back to render aid, or if it was one of the guys in the truck coming back to finish him off.

He hadn't waited around to find out. He'd turned off the dome light to keep it from illuminating when he opened the door and pulled his weapon and Apollo's leash from the console. When he'd discovered the door was jammed, he'd had to fight off a panic attack. After a few blows with his shoulder, it had finally creaked open. Then he and Apollo had slipped into the trees before the man had gotten close enough to see them.

Now he was watching from just inside the tree line about twenty feet from the back of his SUV. Apollo stood next to him, as he waited to see if the man approaching was friend or foe. He didn't even have his phone. It had bounced from the cup holder and was lying somewhere in the darkened Land Rover.

When the man reached the vehicle, he shone the flashlight through the front windshield and then moved to the side to check the back seat. A stray glimmer illuminated the nickel barrel of a pistol. Spence straightened, face now hidden, no longer peering around the tree. This was no Good Samaritan, a passerby willing to interrupt his schedule to see if a fellow motorist needed assistance. This was someone determined to see Alyssa dead. What had happened to her? Had she been able to escape? Or had the men forced her off the road and shot her?

He hadn't heard gunfire, or any kind of commotion, for that matter. But that didn't mean anything. He'd been out cold. There could have been an all-out war, and he wouldn't have known.

Two vehicles approached, headed south on 85. The man crossed his arm in front of him, the weapon pressed between his left elbow and waist. Then he circled back around the front of the SUV to crouch at its right front quarter panel.

Spence took advantage of the noise of the vehicles to slip deeper into the woods, Apollo trotting next to him. The dog appeared unhurt. Except for a monster headache, he was, too. Both were serious answers to prayer.

When everything fell quiet again, he paused. Someone moved through the woods, not far to his right. He held his breath and waited, heart pounding. Were the footsteps growing closer? He squeezed his eyes shut and listened, trying to pinpoint the exact location of the man pursuing him.

The image in his mind wavered, and trees became desert sand broken by sparse shrubs. Instead of woods, damaged mudbrick houses lined a pothole-marked street.

No, not now. Spence opened his eyes wide, ingesting the view around him. Not much light came through the heavy clouds. Even less made its way through the branches above him.

But it was enough. He wasn't in Afghanistan. He was in Alabama, his smashed vehicle sitting somewhere along Interstate 85, and his dog leaning into him, further grounding him to reality. He inhaled a deep, silent breath and forced his heart to slow.

He wasn't out of danger, though. He had no phone, no way to call for help. And he had no transportation, no way to drive himself to safety. His vehicle was toast. He didn't have to be an insurance adjuster to make that determination.

The footsteps changed direction. His pursuer was now moving closer. Had he heard something? Had Spence made a sound as he'd fought to stave off the flashback? Or had a small animal moved through the underbrush, and he'd been too distracted to notice?

Now he heard it, a rustle about six feet away. Definitely an animal. Likely an armadillo.

Spence crept silently in the opposite direction, praying he wouldn't step on any twigs or branches. He didn't want to kill someone tonight, but he would if he had to.

Some distance away, another group of cars sped past. When the engine noise faded, the tension fled his body. Whomever he had heard was moving away.

For several more minutes, he waited, listening. Once confident no one was near, Spence backtracked toward the road. He had to check on Alyssa.

Maybe they hadn't been able to get to her. Maybe she had successfully evaded them long enough to call 911. Or maybe they had forced her off the road, and she'd been able to slip into the woods the same way he had.

Alyssa was smart. She'd foiled two attempts on her life in less than six hours. If she'd been conscious and alert enough to escape her car, she could probably remain hidden long enough for help to arrive.

God, please let her outsmart whoever is after her. Please keep her safe.

When he reached the edge of the woods, he looked both directions. His smashed-up Land Rover was twenty or thirty feet behind him. Alyssa would be somewhere up ahead. Maybe.

Instead of walking in the grassy area, he stayed just inside the woods, paralleling the road. Without knowing how many men were out there, he wasn't letting down his guard. The truck had carried at least two. He wasn't sure about the gold car from which the shots had been fired outside Jim's Garage.

He hadn't gone very far when there was a continuous series of loud rustles to his right. He froze, pistol raised. Something large was barreling through the woods toward him. A person, or maybe two people—someone in pursuit and someone fleeing. Judging from the sound, he was right in their path.

He pulled Apollo behind a tree and slipped in behind him, putting the trunk between himself and whoever or whatever was charging toward them. As he peered around it, someone moved into his line of sight, closing in at a limping run. The figure was smaller, like a woman. *Alyssa?*

A shot rang out and his heart went into his throat. But other than a brief zigzag, the figure continued straight for him. Two more shots and she dropped and rolled.

Spence stepped out, spread his legs and squared his body, pistol raised. A second figure came into view, much larger than the first one. He apparently saw Spence the same time Spence saw him. The man raised his weapon and fired a split second before Spence did, but the shot went wide. Spence's was true.

The man crumpled to his knees and fell

forward, face-first on the ground. Spence waited to see if he would attempt to fire again. He didn't.

After signaling Apollo to stay, Spence dropped the leash and approached slowly. He hadn't wanted to kill anyone, but the man had given him no choice. It was either take him out or let him kill Alyssa. This wasn't the first time he'd taken a life. War was ugly. But pulling the trigger always left him with a knot in his gut and a vague feeling of nausea.

Only after making sure the other man had no pulse did he slide the barrel of his weapon into his waistband. "Come, Apollo."

They both approached Alyssa. As soon as he helped her to her feet, she threw herself into his arms, almost knocking him backward.

He wrapped his arms around her, and she slid hers around his waist, holding him as if she would never let go. He'd held her so many times, but it had been eight long years. It had felt natural then. Now it felt awkward. They had both changed. Or maybe it was because he had changed and she hadn't.

He rested his chin on her head. Awkward or not, she needed him. She apparently needed Apollo, too, because the dog had positioned himself against both of them.

"It was him." She spoke the words against his chest. "The guy at the hospital. The one with the syringe."

"Do you have your phone?"

She shook her head, something he felt rather than saw. "It's in the car. I didn't have time to grab it."

"Same here. Where is your car?"

"About a mile ahead of where you crashed."

"Let's get it. We need to call for help. There's still a guy in the woods, the one who came after me."

She stiffened suddenly. "There's a third one watching my car. When I eluded the first guy, I went back for my phone and almost ran into him."

He frowned. So there were still two men out there hunting them. At least, that they knew of. There could be more in other vehicles. "We'd better hike to the nearest town, see if we can flag down a police cruiser. Someone might see our wrecked vehicles and call the authorities, but waiting around to find out doesn't seem like a good idea."

"We passed Tuskagee two or three miles back."

"We did. Can you make it?"

"I'll make it."

When she dropped her arms, he picked up Apollo's leash and put one hand through the loop. As he straightened, a rustle sounded some distance away. He held up a hand. "Shh."

For several moments, Spence listened, cocking an ear toward the woods. There was definitely movement, but whether someone was walking their way or parallel to the road, he couldn't tell.

"Let's cross. I think we'll be safer on the other side of the interstate."

As soon as there was a good break in traffic on both sides, she hurried with him across the southbound lanes, through the median and to the opposite side of the lanes headed north. Apollo loped ahead of them, leash gently taut. Then they slipped through the edge of the tree line.

A few hours ago, he'd been headed to his apartment, boxes in the back of his SUV, schedule for the next two days neatly laid out, ready to pack up, clean and vacate his apartment before his lease ran out.

If having his plans wrecked, his vehicle totaled and someone trying to kill him didn't put him in a bad mood, thinking about the dead man he'd left in the woods did. So did not even knowing what any of it was about.

He looked over at Alyssa. Her face was in shadow. The little bit of light that reached them from approaching traffic came from behind, and the starlight filtering through the trees was almost nonexistent.

"Tell me what you took. Who did you tick off?"

She crossed her arms and stared straight ahead, her gait even stiffer.

"Come on, Alyssa. I killed a man. I have a right to know."

"I didn't take anything." She emphasized each word. "You automatically assume the worst about me." She heaved a sigh. "That's why I don't want to go back to Pensacola. I'll get the same thing from everybody there—my sisters, the people I went to school with, everybody who knew me growing up." She uncrossed her arms to throw her hands up. "Even the police. Everyone's got the same negative expectations, and that's never going to change."

"If you weren't acting like you're hiding something, I could probably be a little more understanding."

"Okay, I inadvertently saw something I wasn't supposed to see. Now these guys are determined to silence me."

"Why don't you report it, get the police involved?"

"Because I don't trust anybody. I don't know what kind of connections these guys have."

He studied her as she spoke. He was inclined to believe her. Maybe, for once, the trouble she was in wasn't because of her own doing.

After almost two hours of walking, they reached Tuskagee.

Alyssa was limping worse, but she hadn't complained once. She was a tough one. His own limp was almost as pronounced as hers. He'd passed the point of trying to hide it more than an hour ago.

Tuskagee was a quiet, small city, but at almost midnight, there was no activity at all. Finally, a Tuskagee Police Department vehicle approached, and they flagged it down. An officer stepped from the passenger side, Probst, according to his name tag. They explained the events of the day, ending with how Spence had killed one of the men in self-defense.

After instructing the other officer to put out an APB for the pickup truck, Probst turned back to Spence. "I assume reports were filed about the shooting near the garage and the event at the hospital."

"Yes."

"And you can show someone where we'll find this body?"

"I can."

"If you two and your dog don't mind sitting in the back of the patrol car, we'll give you a ride to the scene and have the Macon County Sheriff's deputies meet us out there." Probst frowned. "We'll need to confiscate your weapon until the investigation is over."

"I suspected as much."

After the officer had donned a pair of latex gloves, Spence handed over the Glock, which went into an evidence bag.

At least he had another weapon at home, that one a Colt. If he hadn't, he would have bought one; no way was he leaving Alyssa unprotected.

When they arrived at the wrecked Land Rover, two Macon County Sheriff's cruisers were already there. It didn't take long for Spence to backtrack to where he'd left the man in the woods.

Then he called a tow truck for his vehicle. Once his insurance company opened in the morning, he'd report the accident to them.

Probst took them a little farther down the interstate to Alyssa's car, and as soon as he opened her door, she climbed from the back seat. "I'd like to see if my car is drivable." She limped in that direction. "The doors on the right side probably won't open, and they may leak. But if it's safe to drive, I'd rather not have to rent something."

Spence agreed. The sooner they could get out of there, the safer they would be.

And based on the little bit Alyssa had told him, not leaving a paper trail with a car rental company was probably a good idea.

She pulled her keys from her pocket and slid into the driver's seat. "Since the damage is just on the side, I'm hoping the engine and transmission are fine."

The engine cranked on the first try. As she eased forward, Spence watched, the screech and groan of metal setting his teeth on edge. The major components were apparently okay, but that didn't mean pieces wouldn't fall off in transit.

She turned the wheel slightly to the left, easing the vehicle away from the trees. Once clear, she shifted into Park and stepped out.

"I think we're good to go. I wouldn't try any cross-country trips, but as long as it doesn't shimmy and rattle too much, we should be able to make it to Pensacola."

Spence looked at Probst. One of the Macon County units had already left. The other deputies were in the woods, waiting for crime scene to show up. "Can you guys make sure we get away without being followed?"

"Sure thing."

"Thanks." Meanwhile, he'd look for a route to Pensacola using back roads, in case the men would be watching for them along the interstate. If her car stood out before, it would really stand out now.

After Probst relayed the request, Alyssa crossed her arms, frowning. "When I left Atlanta, I made sure I wasn't followed. When I left LaGrange, the LaGrange Police Department made sure I wasn't followed. But both times, some dangerous people found me. How is that possible?"

Probst pressed his lips together. "Any chance you've got a tracking device?"

Spence nodded. "My thoughts exactly." They were probably Alyssa's, too.

He passed Apollo's leash to Alyssa. Then he and the officer dropped to their knees and slowly worked their way around the

Tempo, inspecting its underside by flashlight.

Alyssa waited at the back bumper. "I'd offer to help, but I have no idea what we're looking for."

Spence wasn't sure he did, either, but he had enough knowledge of mechanics to know when he was looking at something that didn't belong there.

After searching the exterior, including the bumper and grill, Spence moved inside. He'd heard the most common place for GPS trackers was under the dash. Dropping the dash took time, longer than he'd hoped, and didn't produce a tracking device.

Officer Probst met him at the open driver's door. "I have one other idea." He looked at Alyssa. "Is it all right if we remove your taillight covers?"

She lifted her brows. "Are you seriously concerned about doing damage to my car?"

He smiled. "I guess not."

Spence climbed from the car and watched him remove the left cover then the right.

"Bingo."

Spence moved closer. A flat, rectangular object had been connected to the taillight wiring and stuffed into the space.

Alyssa shook her head. Even in the dim light, her face seemed to have lost color. "I have no idea when that was put there, but I want it gone." She looked at Spence. "Can you get rid of it?"

"Without making the taillight inoperable?"

"Preferably."

"Maybe. We'll need to cut the wiring going into the tracking device and splice it."

"Can you do it? I need to be able to drive my car."

At 1:00 in the morning, they weren't likely to find an auto parts store open. "I'll give it a shot."

Thankfully, Alyssa carried a well-stocked tool kit in her trunk. Within twenty minutes, he had the tracking device removed and her taillight functional. The brake light and turn signal even worked.

She gave him a crooked smile. "You're good."

"I know a few things."

After they had both thanked Probst and the other law enforcement personnel who had shown up to see to their safety, Alyssa slid in behind the wheel, and Spence and Apollo climbed into the back seat.

He passed her backpack forward. "If you let me use your phone, I'll look for an alternate route."

After she had handed it to him, she pulled onto the interstate, the sheriff vehicles coming out behind them.

"These guys who are after you, do they know where you're from?"

"No. Any time someone asks, I say Florida. If they want to know where in Florida, I say near Tallahassee."

He quirked an eyebrow. She was apparently using the term "near" loosely. Both towns were in the Panhandle, but they were three hours apart. Her secrecy said a lot about the people she chose to hang around with. Maybe that was at least part of the reason she had changed her name.

Alyssa continued. "But don't worry. I'm not planning to stay. As soon as I can figure out a game plan, I'm out of there."

"You know, there are worse places to be stuck than Pensacola."

"Yeah, Atlanta."

Her voice was heavy with meaning. The trouble she'd found was apparently there. But it wasn't staying there. It was following her wherever she went.

"Please don't leave before I get back."

She didn't respond.

"Let me help, please. Promise me. Don't you at least owe me that?"

Maybe that was low, trying to make her feel obligated. But if it would keep her from running before he got back, it was worth it.

Spence had no control over her actions.

No matter how badly he wanted to make sure she was safe, he couldn't force her to stay.

But one thing was sure.

This time, he wouldn't be the one to walk away.

FOUR

"Alyssa."

Alyssa squeezed her eyes shut more tightly and released a moan. Someone was calling her. It wasn't the first time, either.

"Alyssa, wake up." The voice was deep, but soothing.

"Go away." Her words came out slurred.

Now, a gentle shoulder shake. Why couldn't they just leave her alone?

She opened her eyes. The ceiling was less than two feet from her face. Where was she?

She pushed herself upright, and everything came back to her in a rush. She was in the passenger seat of her Tempo. During their 3:00 a.m. gas stop, she had crawled over the console and allowed Spence to drive. After being awake for a straight twenty-two hours, she had needed a break.

For the next two hours, she had talked with Spence, helping keep him alert until they'd pulled into a rest area along I-10, sixty minutes from her childhood home. At that early hour, she hadn't been willing to call either of her sisters. She hadn't felt like landing on Kris's doorstep at six in the morning, either.

She didn't know what Spence had done, but at that point, she had reclined her seat and fallen promptly to sleep, staying comatose until—

"What time is it?"

"A quarter till eight."

She brought her seatback into a vertical position. Whoa, she had slept almost three hours. They weren't even at the rest area anymore. They were getting ready to enter a McDonald's drive-through.

Spence pulled up to the communication box. "Did you want anything?"

Alyssa looked at the menu board. She

should conserve her cash, but showing up at her sister's house needing to beg for a place to stay was bad enough without having to add, "By the way, I need you to feed me, too."

Spence cranked the window down as a female voice came through the speaker.

"Welcome to McDonald's. May I take your order?" The woman sounded annoyingly perky for seven forty-five in the morning.

While Spence placed his order, Alyssa read the menu choices and settled on a bacon, egg and cheese biscuit. That should tide her over till lunch.

When the woman passed the bag containing their breakfast to Spence, pleasant aromas filled the car and Alyssa's stomach growled. She hadn't eaten since lunch yesterday. During what should have been dinnertime, she'd been stuck at the emergency room. After leaving the hospital, she'd been too focused on trying to stay alive to think about her stomach. Now she was starving. Maybe she should have ordered two breakfast sandwiches.

Once Spence had unwrapped his sandwich and folded back the paper, he pulled onto North Ninth Avenue. A knot formed around the few bites Alyssa had already taken. Her childhood home was only fifteen minutes away.

She'd walked away from her past seven years ago and never looked back. While planning the trip to her mother's memorial service, she had tried to mentally prepare herself. Her one consolation had been that as soon as it was over, she could hightail it back to Atlanta. That was no longer the case. She would be stuck in Pensacola for an indeterminable period of time.

She squared her shoulders and straightened her spine. It was still temporary. Maybe not as temporary as she had originally planned, but as soon as she could get on her feet and figure out a game plan, she would be out of there.

She finished the final half of her biscuit. Although it still tasted good, each bite seemed to lodge somewhere just before reaching her stomach.

Finally, Spence pulled into the driveway and the old Victorian stood in front of her.

It looked much the same as it had when she'd left, just slightly less maintained. Paint that had started to fade almost a decade ago showed even more signs of age, with the parts exposed to full sun a tone of gray several hues lighter than those areas blessed with shade. The accents that had once been burgundy and slate blue looked more like mauve and a bleached-out blue-gray.

But the Victorian was still grand and elegant. She would appreciate it if not for her past. Besides, it was a whole lot better than some of the places she'd lived over the past seven years, which wasn't saying much. If the shutters were cockeyed, the roof sagging and the porch railing gone, it would exceed that bar.

In spite of its need for a couple coats of

paint, the yard looked great. Kris had obviously spruced it up. The lawn was neatly mowed and flowers lined both sides of the curved walk leading from the driveway to the front porch.

Spence killed the Tempo's engine but left the keys in the ignition. "Would you like me to walk up with you?"

"Let me go first."

Her sister wouldn't be thrilled to see her. If she rang the bell with Spence next to her, Kris might shut the door in both of their faces.

Neither of her sisters had liked Spence. They'd probably felt he was a bad influence on her. He probably had been. But she'd been an equally bad influence on him.

Spence opened the door and stepped from the car. Even though he wasn't walking to the door with her, he still had to let her out. Having the entire passenger's side of her car smashed in was a pain in the neck.

She climbed over the console and, when she had slid from the driver's seat, Spence got back into the car. As she made her way up the curved walk, her chest tightened. Why did coming home feel like making the dreaded walk to the principal's office?

After stepping onto the porch, she turned to look back at Spence. He was watching her through the windshield. When her gaze met his, his lips curved upward. He'd always had an infectious smile—ten percent friendliness, ten percent charm and eighty percent mischief. Now it was one hundred percent encouragement.

She squared her shoulders. She could do this, even without Spence's support. It didn't matter that he was moving back to Pensacola and she was stuck there for the time being. She wouldn't get used to someone she couldn't count on.

She lifted her right hand to press the doorbell. As long as she didn't have to use the left, the shoulder didn't bother her too badly. Ten days from now, she would have to have the stitches removed.

Maybe she could get Kassie or Kris to snip them for her and save herself a trip to the doctor. Or maybe she'd go ahead and put the health insurance she had to good use before she lost it at the end of the month.

The lock rattled and Alyssa stiffened. Preparing for a conversation with either of her sisters felt like gearing up for battle. Maybe they felt the same way about her.

The door creaked back on its hinges, and Kris stood in the opening, a golden retriever next to her. There was no hint of surprise on her face. Of course, she had probably peered out one of the windows before opening the door.

Or maybe Kris didn't recognize her. Her hair was longer and a different color. There were probably other changes, too. Although they'd talked on the phone several times, they hadn't seen each other since Alyssa had left. She hadn't come back and, through the years, Kris hadn't made any attempt to go wherever Alyssa had landed.

Kris's gaze flicked over her. "You're a little late, don't you think?"

Yep, Kris recognized her. There was no surprise, but there wasn't any welcome, either.

Alyssa bristled. The resentment she felt toward her older sisters was nothing new. When their mother had disappeared and their father had dived even deeper into the bottle, twins Kassie and Kris had gone off to college a short time later, leaving fifteen-year-old Alyssa to fend for herself. Things had only gone downhill from there. Two years later, Spence had left and they'd gone downhill even faster.

She glanced at Bella who was staring up at her with big brown eyes. The tail moved slowly back and forth. The dog would give her a warmer welcome than her sister would.

Alyssa lifted her chin. She wasn't going

to allow her sister's judgment to beat her down. "I was on my way here yesterday morning, and my car broke down."

And someone tried to kill me...twice.

She left the last thought unspoken. It wouldn't get her any sympathy. Just the opposite. Her sister would assume she'd brought it on herself and have one more reason to judge her.

Kris looked past her and into the driveway.

"I had it repaired." The engine anyway. The body was too far gone. Her insurance company would declare the car a total loss if she had full coverage. She didn't. The best she could hope for was two or three hundred from a salvage yard.

She turned back around to face her sister. "I was planning to spend a couple of weeks in Pensacola and was thinking about crashing at the old homestead."

Kris lifted her eyebrows. "That sounds like an *I need a place to lie low.*"

Kris had hit the nail on the head. How

could she do that when they only talked to each other every few months? Her sisters never called her, except for brief Christmas and birthday greetings, and she only called her sisters when she needed help, like when she'd given her roommate her half of the rent and the woman had blown the entire thing on a shopping spree.

Kris crossed her arms. "Is that your boyfriend in the car?"

Alyssa laughed, a hearty belly laugh that took several seconds to rein in. The thought of Peter behind the wheel of her beat-up Tempo was hilarious. The idea that the man currently there would ever again hold the boyfriend title was even more outrageous.

Before Alyssa could answer the question, a little boy toddled into the foyer and wrapped his arms around Kris's leg.

"Mommy?"

She picked him up and propped him on one hip, his legs resting one in front of her and the other behind. His arms went around her neck.

Alyssa smiled at the little boy. "Hi, Gavin." She did the math in her head. Her nephew was two and a half and she'd never met him.

"Gavin, this is your Aunt Alyssa." Her tone seemed to hold resignation.

"Ann Issa?"

Alyssa's heart swelled at hearing the little boy try to pronounce her name. It was her first glimpse of what she might have missed by running away instead of working to have a relationship with her sisters.

As children, none of them had been close. From what she'd gathered during infrequent conversations with Kassie and Kris, the twins had mended bridges and were actually enjoying a closeness they'd never shared as children.

Alyssa patted his back. "Yeah, buddy. That's me. Aunt Alyssa is going to be in town for a little while. I hope we can do some fun things together."

She liked kids. Not that she ever planned to have any. She'd probably mess things up as badly as her own parents had.

Actually, putting the blame on her mother was unfair. She'd spent so many years hating her mom for leaving them that, even though she now knew otherwise, the thought often slipped through before she had a chance to censor it.

Kris sighed. "I'd like to invite you inside but, frankly, I have my reservations. Whatever trouble you're in, I don't want you bringing it here. I'm telling you right now, I will do everything in my power to protect this little boy. If you and your friend need a place to stay for a few days, I'll pay for a hotel room. Kassie will probably chip in, too." She looked into the driveway again, where just the driver's side and front of the Tempo were visible from their perspective. "Wait a minute. Is that…?" Her brows dipped together.

Spence took the cue and stepped from the vehicle.

Alyssa watched him approach, his easy gait and relaxed smile reminding her far too much of the teenage boy she had fallen in love with.

Kris moved forward. "Hi, Spence."

Alyssa turned back to her sister and did a double take. The defensiveness she'd expected to see wasn't there. Instead, everything about her—from her relaxed posture to her friendly tone to the smile that matched Spence's—exuded welcome.

An unexpected sense of annoyance swelled inside her. Alyssa had known neither of her sisters would roll out the welcome mat for her, but she hadn't expected Spence to get an enthusiastic welcome when her own had been somewhere south of *meh*.

Kris stepped back. "Come on in, you guys. Have you had breakfast?"

Alyssa nodded. "We stopped at McDonald's."

Kris closed the door behind them and

looked at Spence. "You've made your move already?"

So Kris knew about his plans to return to Pensacola. How much had her sisters kept from her?

"I'm working on it. I'm going back to La-Grange today to finish packing and heading back down tomorrow with a loaded U-Haul."

Kris led them into the living room, the golden retriever trotting behind them. After putting Gavin down, she shifted her gaze between them. "How did you guys get reconnected?"

"Her car broke down in LaGrange, and I happened to be driving past the garage as she was coming out."

Coming out? She almost laughed. Running across the road in front of him, dodging bullets, was more like it. The fact that Spence had left it up to her how much she would tell her sister increased the appreciation she already had.

She excused herself to use the restroom

and made her way down the hall. Kris had said she didn't want her bringing trouble there. She had a valid point.

Now that Alyssa had gotten rid of the tracking device, the likelihood of Peter and his cronies following her to Pensacola was slim. But if they did and she was staying in the family home, Kris and Gavin could be caught in the crossfire. It was a chance she wasn't willing to take. She wouldn't even consider it.

When she stepped from the bathroom, hushed voices drifted to her from the direction of the kitchen. As she drew closer, they fell silent. Had Kris and Spence been talking about her? Maybe she'd been premature in the ramped-up appreciation she'd felt earlier.

She stopped in the doorway and leaned against the jamb. "Instead of staying here, I'd like to crash in the apartment over the charter office."

Kris's gaze went immediately to Spence.

What was up with that? He had no say in their family decisions.

After brief hesitation, she lifted her shoulders in a slow shrug and let them fall. "I'll have to talk to Kassie."

"Why? I have as much right to the space as anyone."

The charter company had belonged to their dad. He was now serving time for drug running, with murder likely being added to those charges in the near future. He was also dying. The house, the boats, the business and the building housing it and the one next door would at some point belong to all three of them.

Another glance passed between Kris and Spence.

Yeah, something was going on, something both of them were keeping from her.

Fine. They could talk all they wanted.

As soon as she could get her act together, she'd be gone.

Whatever they said or did then was none

of her concern, because she had no intention of ever coming back.

A powerful explosion rocked the ground, bringing the entire convoy to an abrupt stop. A cloud of dust and debris swallowed the lead vehicle.

Spence gripped the steering wheel of the Joint Light Tactical Vehicle and scanned the landscape on either side of him—miles and miles of rolling desert broken by small patches of scrub. Any of those rises could conceal Taliban fighters.

Seconds ticked by before a barrage of machine gun fire rent the silence. Several shots pinged off the right side of the JLTV.

"Take cover." Spence swung open the door and dropped to the ground, M4 clutched in his right hand.

Three others followed him out, making their way in a crouched run to a berm near the edge of the road.

More artillery fire erupted around them, the attackers taking advantage of their increased vulnerability. Beside him, McCarthy shrieked and dropped to the dusty road, legs bent in a way that didn't look quite natural.

Spence stopped and grabbed his arm. "Come on."

"I can't feel my legs." He screamed the words, the high-pitched tone an amalgamation of panic, pain and terror.

Norris took his other arm and together they pulled him off the road and over the berm at its edge, artillery whizzing past.

The gunfire continued, punctuated by more screams.

The small convoy was outmanned, outgunned and outmaneuvered. The road had supposedly been cleared. One IED had obviously been missed. *God, help us all.*

Something wet moved up Spence's face. Now there was pressure against his side. The screams and gunfire faded, leaving only a soft whimper.

He opened his eyes and the images of war splintered. Instead, a furry brown face hovered close to his own. Apollo whimpered again and followed it with another slurp of his tongue across Spence's cheek.

Spence lifted a hand to scratch his dog's neck. His heart pounded against his rib cage, his pulse rate what it would be after a serious cardio session. His breaths came in shallow pants.

He tried to force both his breathing and his heart to slow. There were no mortars, no mines, no men wielding AK-47s, determined to take him out. He was in Pensacola, ensconced in the apartment over the top of what would soon be his long-dreamed-of music store.

He pushed himself upright and wrapped both arms around his dog. "It's okay, buddy. I'm all right."

At least he would be in a few minutes. With Apollo's help, he was always able to bring himself out of the effects of a nightmare pretty quickly. But that didn't mean he'd be getting back to sleep anytime soon.

He rose from the bed and walked to the

small kitchenette occupying the back corner of the apartment. He didn't bother to turn on any lights. Enough glow from the street below drifted through the sheer-covered French doors for him to find his way around without bumping into anything.

After taking a bottle of water from the minifridge, he moved toward the couch. His guitar sat in the stand next to it, still plugged into the amp.

He'd arrived in town just before noon. It was a day earlier than he'd planned to make his move, but he hadn't needed the extra time. When he'd gotten back to La-Grange, he'd boxed everything up, and Jason had come over early this morning to help him load it all into the U-Haul.

By six tonight, he had returned the rental and found places for all of his belongings. Not that there were many. He'd known his stay in LaGrange would be temporary and had managed to acquire only what he'd needed over the past year.

He hadn't seen Alyssa. He hadn't seen

Kris or Kassie, either. With today being Sunday, Ashbaugh Charters had been closed. Since Kris and Kassie had given him the key when he'd signed the lease a month ago, he hadn't even had to get in touch with them.

He'd told Alyssa he was moving back to Pensacola but hadn't revealed exactly where. If she had known her sisters were his new landlords and he'd be working and living in the space next door to the charter office, she would probably have kept driving rather than stay in Pensacola.

Yesterday, without going into detail why, he'd expressed those same concerns to Kris. She'd agreed to keep his living arrangements secret until Alyssa discovered them for herself.

He sank onto the couch, and Apollo jumped up next to him, laying his head in Spence's lap. After unscrewing the cap on the water bottle, Spence took a long swig. Cold and pure, it tasted good, but it wouldn't do anything as far as relaxing him. One activity would, though.

Without getting up, he reached beside him to grasp the neck of the guitar. From the time he was a teenager, music had been his refuge. Back when he and Alyssa had been together, his biggest dream had been to become a famous rock star. And he'd been well on his way to developing the drug habit to go with it.

Not anymore. Instead of hoping to be the next Mick Jagger or Jon Bon Jovi, he'd spent the past year playing in his church's worship band on Sunday mornings. And alone in his apartment in the middle of the night, trying to chase away the demons of war.

He picked up the guitar, and Apollo moved farther down the couch before resting his head between his paws. He knew the drill.

Spence laid the guitar across his lap, the instrument occupying the space the dog had just vacated, and strummed an

E chord. Several beats later, he closed his eyes, shifting his left hand to finger a C-sharp minor chord. He continued to strum, A then back to E, as he started to sing.

It was one of his favorite worship songs, describing how peace is found in the presence of Jesus. It was a truth he felt down to the deepest part of him.

He moved from "I Speak Jesus" to "Holy Forever" without opening his eyes. When finished, he rose to crank up the amp a little louder. He didn't have to concern himself with disturbing anyone. He was downtown, surrounded by businesses. All of them would be vacant in the middle of the night.

He didn't even have to worry about Alyssa. Kassie would likely agree to let her stay in the apartment over the charter office, but she hadn't moved in yet. When he'd taken Apollo out just before bed, he'd checked the parking lot behind the building as well as the parallel spaces lining Government Street in front. The red Tempo hadn't been in either area.

As soon as he sat back down, he began playing the driving intro of Phil Wickham's "Battle Belongs." Halfway through the song, another sound penetrated the music—something like pounding. He stopped singing and laid his right hand flat across the strings. What had he heard?

It came again, definitely pounding. Judging from the volume, there was some anger behind it. Someone was knocking on the doors leading into his apartment from the balcony overlooking the street.

He spun to face the front wall and peered through the sheers hanging over the double French doors. A figure stood there, fist raised, a dark silhouette against the glow of the streetlights below.

What? The only way to access the balcony was through his apartment or the one next door.

Uh-oh.

He flipped a switch, and the light outside came on. Yep, Alyssa had moved in.

After unlocking the doors, he swung one of them inward. She stood on the balcony, hands on her hips.

"Do you mind? I'm trying—"

The words died on her lips as annoyance morphed to shock. Her eyes widened then narrowed.

"You!"

He winced. She was probably angrier over his not telling her where he would be staying than his waking her out of a sound sleep.

She crossed her arms in front of her. "Kris didn't tell me they had this rented, and she certainly didn't tell me their renter was you."

Yep, he'd awoken her. Her hair flowed over her shoulders in wild disarray. She was dressed in her pajamas—a sleeveless top with Bugs Bunny's face over the words "That's All, Folks!" and coordinating bottoms. The playfulness of her attire was at odds with the anger in her green eyes.

Before he could respond, Apollo pressed past him to lean against her leg.

"Hey, Apollo." She dropped to her knees, wrapped both arms around his dog, and then released him to scratch his cheeks. "It's good to see you again."

After petting and cooing at his dog for a couple of minutes, she looked up at him, her smile fading and her eyebrows dipping downward.

"I like your dog better than you right now."

He caught his spontaneous laugh just as it escaped and tried to disguise it with a couple of coughs. Alyssa always said what she thought and never minced words, something he'd appreciated and often found funny.

Alyssa's frown said she didn't see any humor in the situation. She rose and glared at him.

"During those discussions we had about

your move back to Pensacola, you don't think you should have mentioned you were renting Ashbaugh property, especially when I talked about staying over the charter office?"

"I thought about it but—"

"But thought it would be best to keep me in the dark and then just surprise me with it."

"If I had told you where I was staying and my renewed connection with your family, would you have come back? Be honest, Alyssa."

She pressed her lips together, and her eyes dipped to the concrete floor of the balcony. A long span of uneasy silence passed.

Finally, she looked at him. "Probably not. I would have tried to figure out something else."

"That's why I did it. I saw your hesitation when I said I was coming back to Pensacola. I didn't want you taking off and trying to deal with this on your own."

"I don't like being lied to."

"I didn't—"

She cut him off with a raised hand. "You didn't outright lie, but you withheld information."

He raised his eyebrows. That was what she'd been doing from the moment they'd run into each other outside Jim's Garage.

Realization flashed across her features, and her lips turned up in a sheepish smile. "Okay. Fair enough."

"You're staying, right? At least for the time being?"

"You're going to keep it down, refrain from middle-of-the-night concerts?"

"Absolutely." He grew serious. "As much as you don't want to, I hope you'll stay until we know for sure you're out of danger. I'm not law enforcement like your future brother-in-law, but I have a weapon, and after seven years in the military, I know how to use it."

Of course, she knew that. She'd already

watched him shoot one man. It still bothered him and would for a while.

But he had no doubt. If put in the same situation, he'd do it again.

In a heartbeat.

FIVE

Alyssa made her way down the narrow stairway and into the charter office lobby, elastic brace just below the hem of her jean shorts. Her knee was doing better, as long as she restricted herself to flat surfaces.

Stairs, not so much. She'd quickly figured out that leading with the right foot going down and the left going up was the only way she could manage.

Currently, no one was at the desk, but voices drifted down the hall from what used to be her dad's office. Kris was apparently with this afternoon's charter customers, taking care of the paperwork. Kassie was already at the marina with Buck, their captain.

Yesterday evening, Alyssa had had Kris

drop her off at the charter office. Kassie had agreed to let her stay in the pseudo apartment above. Pseudo, because it was nothing more than glorified storage space. The dusty old boxes were still stacked against the wall.

There wasn't even a kitchen or bathroom up there. A trip to the toilet in the middle of the night involved navigating the steep, narrow stairway.

At least the space upstairs had a bed, left from when Kris had stayed for a short time when her own life had been in danger. She'd come out of the experience unharmed…and engaged. The latter had happened the day before she'd arrived.

Alyssa stepped out the front door without disturbing the business going on in the office. The fact that her sisters had even had to discuss whether or not she could stay in the space still irked her. As if she was required to have permission to use something that was one-third hers.

To make matters worse, they'd conspired against her, keeping Spence's living arrangements secret, making her feel like the outsider she'd always been. Alyssa—the black sheep, the one who'd never belonged in the Ashbaugh family.

Of course, Spence had already explained his reasons. He'd been right. She would have tried to go it on her own. In fact, maybe Kris's having to get Kassie's okay to allow her to stay above the charter office had been nothing more than a way to delay her move until Spence was already settled in.

As she stepped onto the sidewalk, she pulled her phone from the back pocket of her shorts and navigated to the Uber app. Yesterday, she had ditched the Tempo.

Maybe she'd been a bit premature. But her first night back home, thinking about her car sitting in the driveway next to Kris's Honda CR-V, an overwhelming sense of dread had kept her awake for most of the night. No matter how many times she'd told herself Spence had found and removed the only tracking device, she hadn't been able to shake the uneasy feeling that Peter would somehow find a way to use the car to locate her.

Her fears weren't far-fetched. There weren't many 1992 Tempos on the road sporting her paint job. There were even fewer with her paint job *and* the whole right side smashed in.

So, yesterday, she'd contacted a salvage yard and recouped the two hundred dollars she had spent at Jim's Garage plus a little extra. Not having a car for the short time she'd be there would be an inconvenience, but if she moved to a large city with public transportation, she wouldn't need one anytime in the near future.

She cast a glance toward the retail space adjoining Ashbaugh Charters. There was a sign in the window that she hadn't noticed last night. Block letters spelled out Cavanaugh Music Center, with Coming Soon in script below.

Spence was sitting at a desk, the only

piece of furniture in the large front room. A laptop sat open in front of him, and Apollo lay on the floor next to him. Like last night, he wasn't in his vest. Maybe he only wore it when they went out.

Before she could return her attention to her app, Spence looked up and waved. She made her way to the door and swung it open, even though she was probably going to regret it. She had no interest in getting chummy with her ex.

Chances were good he felt the same way about her. He had changed in the past eight years. He was no longer a youth with no discipline, no direction. Now he exuded maturity, the sense that he'd managed to somehow get his life together when she was still trying to find all the broken pieces of hers.

Yeah, Spence was probably like her sisters—afraid if he spent too much time with her, some of that *worthless* might rub off.

She stepped inside. "Hey."

"Hey, yourself." He flashed her the smile that had always had a way of undoing her.

She refused to be affected. She appreciated everything he was doing for her. Someday she would pay him back for all of it.

She was keeping tabs. So far, she owed him an insurance deductible on his SUV. And a tank of gas when he'd slid his credit card into the slot on the pump while she'd gone inside to pay cash. And any car rental costs he might be stuck with until his insurance claim was over. No way was she going to allow herself to become obligated.

She let the door swing shut behind her. "You look like you're making big plans."

A legal pad lay next to the computer, a pen placed diagonally across it. Several lines were filled with his jagged script, but, from her vantage point, she couldn't make out what he had written. His wallet was also there, sitting on the other side of his computer.

"I am. Right now, I'm ordering inventory."

"For Cavanaugh Music Center."

"Yep. I'm starting out with guitars, keyboards, amps, mixers, mics, et cetera. Maybe eventually I'll even do lessons out of here."

"Wow." He was putting down deep roots. It didn't matter, because she wasn't.

"Sorry I disturbed you last night. When I went to bed, your car wasn't there, so I figured you were still at Kris's."

"I scrapped the car. I had planned to trade it in soon anyway, but my fight with the trees along 85 sped that up a little bit."

His gaze dipped to the hem of her shorts. "How is your knee?"

"Better. I can almost walk now without limping."

"That's good."

"I'm not ready for any long hikes yet. I'm getting ready to Uber to Publix. Kris took me shopping on the way here last night, but now that I've done some meal planning, I have a few other things to pick up."

Spence closed the laptop and stood. "I'd planned on doing some grocery shopping this afternoon, too. How about riding along?"

She hesitated. "You were going anyway?"

He slid his wallet into the front pocket of his jeans. "Absolutely."

"In that case, I'll save the Uber fare."

After locking the front door, he led her out the back and into the parking lot, Apollo next to them. None of the vehicles looked familiar except Kris's red CR-V.

Spence clicked the key fob, and lights flashed on a charcoal-gray Subaru Forester. He opened the passenger door and Alyssa climbed inside. While he waited for Apollo to hop into the back seat, she looked at him over her shoulder. "Any word yet on what they're doing with your Land Rover?"

"Not yet." He closed her door and circled the vehicle to slide into the driver's seat. "The adjuster is supposed to be looking at it today, so I should know something soon. I'll be really surprised if they don't total it."

"I'm sorry. I feel bad." She really did. He was probably regretting stopping to help her.

"Hey, don't worry about it. That's what insurance is for."

Five minutes later, Spence pulled into the grocery store parking lot. By the time they'd made it through produce, her knee was beginning to throb.

As she and Spence and Apollo started down the soup aisle, two older ladies entered the aisle from the other end. Alyssa recognized both of them as former neighbors. Dorothy had lived across the street, Mildred a few doors down. As they passed, Mildred greeted them with a friendly hello. Dorothy offered her own greeting, but her features were tight.

Alyssa stopped in front of the selection of soups. After placing a chicken noodle and a vegetable beef into her cart, she picked up a can of clam chowder. Dorothy's voice came from the next aisle. "Let's hope they're just passing through."

"Why?"

"Those two were always trouble."

Alyssa clenched her teeth. Did the woman think those shelving units were soundproof, or had she intended for them to hear her?

"That was years ago. A lot of teenagers get off to a rough start then get straightened out once they hit adulthood. I don't know what Alyssa's been up to, but Spence enlisted in the military."

"Well, you know what they say. The apple doesn't fall far from the tree. Bobby Ashbaugh is doing time for drug running. No telling what his kids are involved in."

"Hey." Mildred's tone held a definite

hint of scolding. "I babysit for one of those young ladies, so don't be making judgments."

"That would be Kris. Kassie turned out all right, too." Dorothy's voice faded as they moved farther down the aisle. "Those two always kept their noses clean, but with the younger one, I'll believe it when I see it." Any further conversation didn't reach them.

Alyssa glared at Spence. "See why I don't want to stay here? I'll be judged everywhere I go."

"The one lady defended you guys."

"That was Mildred. Of course she's going to stick up for us. She's sort of employed by my sister."

"Don't let it bother you."

That was easy for him to say. His military experience would redeem him in the eyes of everyone who knew his past. She didn't have any acts of heroism to fall back on.

When they finished their shopping, she

hobbled to the nearest cashier, Spence behind her.

"You're limping more."

She looked at him over one shoulder. "I know. If I'd had to navigate many more aisles, you'd have had to wheel me around in the cart."

Spence laughed. Whether he'd actually been planning to grocery shop today or had just told her that so she'd accept his offer, he'd made good use of the time. His cart was more than half full.

Hers was a little skimpier, but not by much. She had watched her spending, taking advantage of the BOGOs. The buy-one-get-one deals had saved her about twenty bucks.

She wasn't quite as worried about her money running out. Besides the two thousand dollars she'd squirreled away in recent weeks, she now had a job. Ashbaugh Charters had recently lost its part-time clerical person. Kassie and Kris had agreed to stop their search and put Alyssa on the payroll while she was there. The offer hadn't even come with any sighs or eye rolls. Maybe there was hope yet the three of them would one day be close. She wasn't counting on it.

When they stepped outside, Spence pointed at a table piled high with cookies, set up not far from the door. They'd passed it on their way into the store. "Dessert. Gotta support the Girl Scouts."

Two young girls manned the table, each wearing a vest sporting more than a dozen embroidered patches. One was talking with a customer who had just purchased a box of Caramel deLites. As they approached, the other girl aimed some baby talk at Apollo and then smiled at his two humans. "How can I help you?"

Spence scanned the offerings. After choosing a box of Caramel Chocolate Chip cookies, he turned to Alyssa. "Which one would you like?"

"I'm going to get the Thin Mints."

"I've got it." He took the box from her

and handed both of them to the Girl Scout to bag.

She frowned at him. "I can pay for my own cookies."

"Trust me, I'll make you share them with me."

As Spence counted out bills, the other customer turned and started to nod a greeting. Then her eyes widened. "Alyssa?"

"Brandi."

The woman had been one year behind her in school and looked much the same now as she had back then, with wispy blond hair and an open, warm smile that made everyone feel as if they were her best friend. Alyssa had known her well, but it had been Brandi's older brothers who had hung around with her and Spence, along with whatever girlfriends they'd had at the time.

Brandi's smile widened. "I like the red. It looks good on you."

"Thanks. You look great, too."

"And Spence." Brandi waved an index

finger between the two of them. "Are you guys...?"

"No." They answered simultaneously, and Spence continued. "We just ran into each other two days ago."

"And who is this?" Brandi bent over but stopped short of petting Apollo.

Spence dipped his head toward his dog. "This is Apollo."

"Is it okay if I pet him?"

"Sure."

After a few minutes of catching up, Spence asked about her brothers.

"Braydon works for Pensacola PD, and Bryson is with Escambia County Sheriff's Office."

What? The Feldman brothers had gotten into even more trouble than she and Spence had. Now they were cops?

Alyssa sighed. And Spence had spent seven years serving his country and was getting ready to open his own music store. Apparently, all of the old gang had made something of themselves.

Well, almost all.

She hoisted the thin strap of her purse up farther on her shoulder. "Are any of you guys married, have families?"

"Nope, and Mom's having a fit. At twenty-four, twenty-five and twenty-six, we were supposed to have given her grand-children by now."

Brandi pulled her phone from her purse. "I've got to take a selfie. Braydon and Bryson aren't going to believe this."

She dropped to her knees next to Apollo, and Alyssa bent forward behind her. She wouldn't be doing any kneeling for a while.

Once Spence had positioned himself in a squat on Apollo's other side, Brandi handed him the phone. "Here, you've got longer arms."

When he had captured some photos he was happy with, he handed the phone back to Brandi.

Alyssa peered at the screen. "Can you text me one of those?"

"Sure."

A few seconds after Alyssa gave Brandi the number, her phone buzzed with an incoming text, but Brandi was still typing. Finally, she slid her phone back into her purse.

"Now Braydon and Bryson have it, too, along with the message *Guess who I ran into*."

Brandi's phone dinged with a notification.

Alyssa tensed, dread trickling over her. "Did you just post that to social media?"

"I did. Why?"

"Please delete the post." She didn't even try to keep the panic from her voice.

"O-kay." Brandi pulled her phone from her purse and opened the app. After a few more taps, she looked back at Alyssa. "Done. I'm sorry. I should have asked."

Alyssa sucked in a stabilizing breath, trying to slow the beating of her heart, which suddenly felt as if it was going to pound right out of her chest. "I'm hiding from an abusive ex."

She would never have described him as abusive before. He'd always been just the opposite, spoiling her every chance he got. But since he'd tried to kill her twice—or had sent someone else to do it—the label fit.

She continued. "I deleted my profile, but I'm not willing to take any chances of him seeing a post and tracking me down."

"I understand. If it'll make you feel any better, my phone is set to not collect location metadata, and I didn't tag a location on the post." She smiled. "Single girls can't be too careful." She turned her attention to Spence. "My brothers are going to want to see you. The last we knew, you had joined the army."

"I had, but I'm out now, as of a year ago."

"Can I get your phone number?"

Alyssa only half listened to their conversation, the social media post overshadowing everything else.

It had been up for only a minute. There was no way Peter could have seen it during that brief time, even if he was friends with every one of her former acquaintances. She couldn't even remember if she had ever received or accepted a friend request from Brandi.

After they said their goodbyes, Alyssa walked with him toward the Subaru, thankful an ice pack was only a few minutes away. She had long ago passed the point of needing to elevate her leg. Spence was having his own issues, evident by how heavily he was leaning against the handle of the cart. Maybe someday she would feel comfortable asking him how he had hurt himself.

They each loaded their groceries into the back, and Alyssa climbed into the passenger seat, a vague sense of worry chewing at her peace of mind. For Peter to have seen the post, he would have had to be watching Brandi's account twenty-four-seven. He was far too busy and powerful.

That wasn't any consolation. He was too busy to stare at social media accounts for hours on end, but he had people. Three of them had already come after her. One was dead. How many more were there?

Spence cranked the engine and pulled from the lot. When they reached the parking area behind the Ashbaugh building, he didn't make a move to get out of the SUV. Instead, he turned toward her.

"I know Publix is only five minutes from here, but you haven't said a word since we told Brandi goodbye."

She shrugged. "I've got a lot on my mind."

"I'm sure you do. Maybe it's time to get it *off* your mind. You told me you don't know who is trying to kill you, but you told Brandi you're hiding from an abusive ex. It can't be both, and I'm guessing it's not either."

Alyssa crossed her arms. She didn't need

his judgment, and she didn't need him trying to fix her life.

"Come on, Alyssa. I want to help, but you need to tell me what's going on."

"You can't help. I need to just leave. I'm going to buy a bus or airline ticket to a big city and disappear."

Before Spence could respond, Apollo climbed from the back seat to lay his upper body along the length of the console. Then he rested his head against Alyssa's shoulder.

The flesh there was still tender, but she didn't care. She would take Apollo's comfort any time. He seemed to be picking up on her agitation and offering his calming presence. Was that what he did for Spence? She'd assumed the dog assisted him with whatever physical limitations he had from his injuries, because he seemed too put together to need emotional support. But maybe she wasn't the only one of the old gang who still struggled.

She cupped the dog's chin and pressed her cheek to the top of his head.

"Alyssa?"

When she didn't respond, Spence laid his hand on the side of her head. He couldn't rest it on her shoulder because the dog had claimed that spot.

She closed her eyes. Spence's touch stirred her far more than she wanted to admit. She wanted to hate him, or at least to still hang on to the resentment she had carried for the past eight years.

But that resentment had begun fading during the trip to the hospital. In its place, other things had started to slip in, things she didn't want to feel—tenderness, affection, need.

He let his hand slide off her head, catching strands of hair between his fingers. "I just want to see you safe and…" His voice trailed off.

Yeah, he probably wanted to see her happy, too. And settled.

"Please let me be there for you."

Because you weren't eight years ago?

She lifted her face from Apollo's head, leaving the words unspoken.

Letting him be there for her sounded pretty good, even though everything within her rebelled at the thought. Somebody she could trust to help her figure this whole thing out and somehow find a way out of the mess she'd fallen into. Somebody who could carry the burden, just for a while, and give her a break.

"I told you before that I saw something I wasn't supposed to see." The words spilled out, slipping through a breach in the wall she had built around her heart. Letting him into her life, even in a small way, felt like waving the white flag of surrender.

"Thursday night, I was out with my boyfriend." *Was it really just four nights ago?* It seemed like a lifetime. "We had gone out to dinner." The restaurant was one of those places where the cost of dinner was equivalent to a week's salary. Her salary, anyway.

"We had just left the restaurant when Peter got a call. He changed routes and eventually stopped at a row of storefronts downtown and told me to wait in the car. I did, for about twenty minutes. After that, I started to get antsy. It wasn't a great part of town, and I was pretty annoyed he'd left me sitting out there alone all that time."

In hindsight, she should have just stayed put, however long it took. It hadn't been the first time impatience had gotten her into trouble. But it had been the most serious.

"I got out and went into the building. The front of the space was vacant, but I could hear voices coming through an open door to a back room. They were talking about famous paintings." She knew some of the pieces—*Henriette de France, Lady Caroline Price, Marjorie In A Yellow Shawl.* "Peter is an art aficionado, and I recognized several of the names they mentioned as paintings he has."

She took in a deep breath.

Spence didn't ask questions and didn't prod her, just quietly listened.

"When I stepped into the open doorway, three men were sitting around a table with Peter, passing photos around. From where I was standing, I couldn't see what they were looking at, but one of the men said, 'This one is exactly what one of Bud's contacts is looking for.' He said to go ahead and make the arrangements, usual drop-off point, all cash."

She shook her head. "I thought they were dealers of fine art until one of the men looked up and saw me standing in the doorway."

The look he'd given her had sent a chill down her spine. Even now, a shudder shook her shoulders.

"The other two looked up then, and Peter turned around. His back had been to me. I knew instantly I wasn't supposed to be there. I apologized for interrupting, told them I was going to use the restroom but could wait. I hurried back to the car, and

Peter came out right behind me. While he was taking me home, his phone rang. I couldn't hear the caller's words, but Peter said, 'Don't worry. I'll take care of it' and hung up."

She stopped talking and stroked Apollo's head, which was still pressed against her shoulder.

"He tried to convince me everything was on the up-and-up, that these guys were very protective of their work and I had just startled them." It might have been convincing if she hadn't been so street smart. "Anyhow, he knew I was leaving for my mother's funeral the next morning, so when he dropped me off at home, he insisted on taking me, afraid my car wouldn't make it to Florida."

She smiled over at him. "That concern was legitimate. But I knew in my gut if I got into his Audi the next morning, wherever I landed, it wouldn't be Mom's service. So I got up before daybreak, stuffed what I could into my backpack and disappeared. Got as far as LaGrange." She gave him a wry smile. "And, as they say, you know the rest of the story."

Spence released a slow whistle. "You've really landed in hot water. You need to report what you saw to the Atlanta police."

"And tell them what? All I have is an overheard conversation. There wasn't even any art in the building. I'm sure those photos they were passing around went with them. Even if the art they were talking about was stolen, I have no proof."

"How about talking to Jared and Tony?"

"No way." Jared was Kassie's fiancé and Tony was Kris's, and they were both cops. "Peter is a successful man, with enough money to wear designer suits, buy expensive cars and outfit whatever current girlfriend he has in a brand-new wardrobe." She'd fallen for all of it, hook, line and sinker. "Money equals power. And power equals connections."

Going to the police was the first thing she'd thought of. Then she'd dismissed the idea as soon as it had crossed her mind. "He's likely to have close friends or family members on the police force."

"These men are just as likely to track you down somewhere else as here. You're safest where you've got friends and family members watching your back. In the meantime, how about if we talk to Jared and Tony? They'll be discreet. They'll do whatever they need to do to keep you safe." He grinned. "They have extra incentive. If you get hurt, they'll have to answer to their future wives."

"That may not be the deterrent you think it is."

No, that wasn't fair. Neither Kassie nor Kris would want anything bad to happen to her. Sometimes they didn't like her, but they'd always loved her.

"All right. I'll talk to my sisters and have them set up times for us to meet with each of the guys."

Maybe that was a mistake. But maybe

not involving the police would be a mistake, too.

Staying might be a bad decision. So might running.

Because she couldn't shake the feeling that no matter what she did or where she went, Peter would somehow find her.

SIX

Spence turned into a driveway and killed the Subaru's engine as Alyssa stared through the front windshield. She'd never been here before. Kassie had bought the ranch-style home three years ago. It was much smaller than the old Victorian they'd grown up in right on Bayou Texar. But it was cute, with its red-brick façade and white front porch.

It also overlooked one of the dozens of Pensacola parks, this one in the North Hill Historic District. It had been one of Alyssa's favorites, with its rose garden, concrete paths, porch swing and white gazebo.

Tonight, though, she wasn't appreciating the park. In fact, she didn't even want to be there. She had agreed to have Kassie and Kris line up times for Spence and her to meet with their guys to get some guidance regarding the mess she was in with Peter. But instead of two one-on-one meetings, Kassie had decided it was a perfect excuse for them to all get together.

It had taken three days to coordinate a time convenient for everyone, but now Alyssa would be stuck sitting through a pseudo family reunion. She hadn't been close to either of her sisters growing up. Although two years wasn't a large spread as adults, during childhood, it had meant different activities, a different circle of friends and often different schools.

She looked over at Spence. "Might as well get this over with."

He gave her a gentle shake. "You make it sound like you're headed to sentencing or something."

"That isn't too far off."

In recent years, the distance between her and her sisters had only grown larger. The few times she had contacted her sisters, she'd had no other choice. When her roommate had spent the rent, Kassie and Kris had grudgingly chipped in so she wouldn't end up sleeping in the park. She now had enough socked away to pay them back but was currently afraid to let go of it.

Contacts from either of her sisters were just as rare. Aside from Christmas and birthday wishes, they only called her when there was something earth-shattering to share—the discovery of their mother's body, the details of her memorial service, their father's cancer diagnosis, Kassie's kidnapping. It hadn't seemed to take either of her siblings long to forget how she had jumped in, willing to put her own life in danger to save her sister.

Spence gave her another gentle shake. "Come on. No one's going to judge you. Let's go inside."

She stepped from the SUV as Spence opened the back door for Apollo. Although he was still driving the Subaru, car shopping was going to be in his near future. He'd gotten a call from the adjuster shortly before they'd left home. They were totaling the Land Rover.

Alyssa shut the door and crossed in front of Kris's CR-V. Kassie's Sorento was sitting in the drive, too. If Tony was there, he'd apparently ridden with Kris. Jared's cruiser was parked in his grandmother's driveway next door, meaning he had probably walked over. According to Kassie, he had moved in when his grandmother was recovering from a broken hip, had met Kassie and never left.

Apollo trotted ahead of them and climbed the three steps onto the porch. Alyssa rang the bell and, moments later, the door swung inward. Kassie wrapped Alyssa in a hug that caught her off guard. She couldn't remember ever being hugged by either one of her sisters. Maybe Kassie hadn't forgotten about Alyssa's selfless act of bravery after all.

Kassie released Alyssa and turned to

Spence. "It's good to see you again. And this must be Apollo. Is it okay if I pet him?"

"Sure."

She dropped to her knees. "Hey, buddy." After giving him some scratches on the cheeks and neck, she straightened. "Come on in. Everyone's hanging out around the grill."

Alyssa followed her through living room and into the kitchen, Apollo and Spence trailing behind. Pleasant aromas wrapped around her and her stomach growled. Two packs of hamburger buns sat on the counter, a variety of condiments lined up beside them. A covered casserole dish was there, too, next to a bowl. Judging from what she could see through the plastic wrap on top, the bowl possibly contained potato salad. If Kris had brought it, it would have been made from scratch.

The tantalizing scents, though, were probably coming from the backyard. Kris and her fiancé were visible through the nine panes of glass making up the top portion of the door.

Even after seven years, she recognized Tony. He and his family had had countless meals at the Ashbaugh home during the time their fathers had been business partners. It had all come to a screeching halt when they'd split on rather unfriendly terms. Soon the Ashbaugh and Sanderson families would be joined once again, this time through marriage.

When they stepped outside, Apollo followed, looking around at the strangers there. Kris's little boy was running around the yard, a toy airplane in his hand, and a man Alyssa didn't recognize stood at the grill holding a long-handled spatula. That was apparently Jared, Kassie's fiancé.

After introductions had been made, Jared transferred the burgers from the grill to a platter and led everyone inside. The two couples joined hands and then reached across the space to form a circle, unbroken only by Alyssa and Spence. Spence took

Kassie's hand in one of his and Alyssa's in the other. Alyssa allowed Tony to take her free hand.

That was a blast from the past. When they were kids, mealtime in the Ashbaugh house had always begun with everyone joining hands and someone saying grace. That someone was usually their mom. On rare occasions, their dad had muttered a few words. Once their mother had disappeared, prayer stopped.

A lot of things had changed that night. Their father, who had never been allowed to drink at home, had spent increasingly more of his evenings and weekends drunk. Kris, who'd always been a bit moody, had been even harder to get along with, and Kassie had spent hours closed up in her room, crying.

Alyssa hadn't been moody or sad. She'd just been angry and had worked out her anger by rebelling against everything her mother had stood for, including her faith. She'd run as far and as fast in the opposite direction as she'd been able. Spence had been happy to accommodate her.

Until he'd decided to take off, too.

The others echoed Jared's "Amen," and Kris moved to the counter to take the lid off the casserole dish. It held baked beans with strips of bacon adorning the top.

After pushing a large spoon into the edge, she peeled back the plastic wrap on the bowl. "Mom's potato salad recipe."

Kassie smiled. "Mom made the best potato salad."

Alyssa would have nodded agreement, but she was too stalled out by the conversation. In the weeks following their mother's disappearance, none of them had spoken of her. Their father hadn't allowed it. When he wasn't around, if they'd spoken of her at all, it hadn't been with affection.

Of course, that had changed when they'd learned the truth, that she hadn't left them by choice. Being several hundred miles away and wrapped up in her own life,

Alyssa hadn't had the opportunity to digest everything the way her sisters had.

After dumping a bag of chips into a bowl, Kassie stepped back. "Grab a plate and dig in."

Spence led Apollo to the other side of the room to lie down. He'd already fed him before they'd left. The dog was well-behaved enough to lie there throughout the meal, never once considering begging.

Alyssa picked up a paper plate, glad for the casual, relaxed atmosphere. Not that the evening would be easy, but at least she wouldn't be sitting stiffly, eating gourmet food from her grandmother's china.

After pouring tea into one of the plastic cups of ice, she headed for the dining room. Soon the seven of them were sitting around the table, plates full and conversation lighthearted. Tony and Jared alternated telling stories that could have been taken right from an episode of *America's Dumbest Criminals*. Soon Alyssa found herself relaxed and laughing with the others.

At a lull, Tony looked at Alyssa, now serious. "Kris said you had some things going on and wanted to get Jared's and my input."

Her chest tightened as the dread she'd arrived with swept back over her. She laid down her burger and wiped her hands on the paper napkin in her lap.

"I stumbled on something that has put my life in danger, and I'm not sure what to do about it."

She relayed everything she had told Spence on Monday while her future brothers-in-law listened without interrupting. When she had finished, she leaned back in her chair. "Now they're determined to do whatever necessary to keep me quiet. My first inclination is to run to a big city and disappear, but Spence is afraid that with these guys' connections, they'll find me."

Tony nodded. "I'm inclined to agree. The safest place for you is right here where you've got friends and family, and we can all keep an eye on you."

Alyssa frowned. Those friends he'd mentioned, she had lost contact with a long time ago. And family...well...

She shifted her gaze from him to Kris. Her mouth was set in a straight line, her eyes slightly narrowed. Alyssa knew the expression.

"Don't look at me like that."

Kris lifted her brows. "Like what?"

"Like *Alyssa's in trouble again. Par for the course.*"

Kris's eyes narrowed even further. "I was looking at you with concern."

Alyssa crossed her arms. "I know I haven't always made the wisest decisions, but for once, the trouble I'm in isn't because of poor choices."

Well, maybe Peter had been a poor choice, but it had been a trap anyone could have fallen into. There was a reason she'd thought he was too good to be true. She should have listened to her gut.

Jared cleared his throat. "Based on what

you overheard, it sounds like these guys might be fencing stolen art."

Tony nodded. "Or maybe even pushing quality reproductions as the real thing."

Yeah, those were the same ideas she had come up with on her own. Now for what to do about it. "Whatever he's involved in, he's making good money at it." And he wasn't about to let his cushy way of life go. The sprawling home he lived in, filled with expensive art and collectibles, the brand-new sports car, the yacht he'd taken her out on two weekends ago, moored at a marina near Savannah—those weren't cheap. And probably not financed with money he made working as a photographer.

She should have seen through it. She liked to think she was smarter than that. Not in this case. Going out with Peter had been the worst decision she had ever made.

But beating herself up wouldn't accomplish anything toward getting her out of the mess she was in.

Jared continued. "I know you're concerned about what kind of connections these guys might have, but I think it would be good to get the police to look into the situation. In fact, a guy I went through the academy with now works for Atlanta PD. How about if I talk to him, tell him the situation, let him know your concerns?"

"I don't know." She still wasn't convinced. "I don't really know anything. Not for sure, anyway. And I certainly don't have any evidence."

"You can give them a good starting point for their investigation—Peter and the vacant storefront. As long as this guy is free, your life is in danger."

She heaved a sigh of resignation. "All right. Go ahead and talk to him."

"Will do." Jared rose from the table. "I'm going to have to cut out. My shift starts in thirty minutes, so I've got about fifteen to get into my uniform and grab Justice."

"Justice?"

"My K9 partner."

"What breed?"

"German shepherd."

A pang of jealousy stabbed through her. Kris had Bella and Kassie would soon enjoy Justice's company. Technically, the dog probably belonged to the Pensacola Police Department, but Kassie would get to love on him whenever Jared was home.

Alyssa had always loved dogs, and the more she was around Apollo, the more she wanted one for herself. Someday.

Kassie walked Jared to the door. Their words drifted back into the dining room—Kassie's "Stay safe," followed by Jared's "I will. Love you," and Kassie's return endearment.

Alyssa was happy to see both of her sisters so much in love, in spite of the sense of longing settling in her chest. She couldn't say she had loved Peter. The relationship had been too new. It had taken her a lot longer than six weeks to drop her guard to the point of handing someone her heart.

A more apt description of her relationship with Peter was that she'd been dazzled by him. He had the kind of exotic good looks that turned heads—strong, masculine features, jet-black hair, equally dark eyes and olive skin. She'd been impressed with his wealth, how he'd carried himself, the way he'd exuded class and confidence. How, whenever they'd been out together, he'd acted as if nothing else mattered.

It had all been an act.

As the front door thudded shut, a phone's ringtone started up somewhere in the house.

Kassie's "Hello?" came moments later. She stepped into the dining room, eyebrows drawn together. "Who's calling?"

Her gaze shifted to Alyssa and stayed there. Alyssa's chest tightened around a ball of uneasiness. Who would be calling her on Kassie's phone?

Kassie lowered the phone and held it

against her abdomen. "A Rachel Osborn is trying to reach you."

Rachel, her coworker at La Maison, the one who had gotten her the job. Alyssa's uneasiness intensified. Right before destroying her phone, she'd sent Rachel a text asking her to let management know she wouldn't be coming back after her mother's service after all. But she hadn't indicated where she was going. She hadn't known herself. So how had Rachel found her?

She took the phone from Kassie and pressed it to her ear with a tentative "Hello?"

"Alyssa?" Yep, definitely Rachel. Born in Alabama, she had the heavy Southern accent to prove it. "I can't believe I got a hold of you."

Alyssa closed her eyes as a wave of dread washed over her. What if Peter was with Rachel? Maybe tracking her down had been his idea.

"I remembered your name was Ashbaugh back when we worked at Joe's Kitchen, and I figured there'd be a lot fewer Ashbaughs than Andersons. But I still contacted a good half dozen before coming across Ashbaugh Charters. You never said anything about your family owning a charter company."

So she'd found her through Ashbaugh Charters; Kassie probably had calls forwarded to her phone. Rachel was the only person Alyssa still associated with who'd known her before she'd changed her name. She should have thought of that.

Alyssa rose from the table, no longer able to remain seated. "Is something wrong?"

"I'm not sure, but I saw something I felt I needed to tell you about. Have you had any contact with Peter since you left?"

Hearing his name sent another wave of dread over her, as if speaking it aloud would somehow conjure him up. She squelched an irrational urge to duck under the table.

"No. Why?"

As Rachel talked, Alyssa walked to the living room and began to pace. Spence followed her, Apollo right behind him.

"He came into La Maison last night. I was the one who waited on him. He was alone, had his iPad with him."

Alyssa stopped her pacing. That had been a regular occurrence before they'd even started dating. Two or three times a week, he would be there for his evening meal, sitting alone, alternating between watching the activity around him, eyes alert, and working on his tablet. Why would Rachel be calling to tell her that?

"Yes?"

"At one point, there was a photo on his iPad—three people and a dog. Looked like a selfie. I just gave it a quick glance, but I'm almost positive the person in the middle was you."

Alyssa sank onto the couch and dropped her head, pressing her palm over her eyes. *No, no, no.* He couldn't have seen the photo. It had only been posted for a minute or two.

A wet nose nudged her hand away. When she opened her eyes, Apollo's furry brown face was inches from her own. Beyond him, Spence stood, frowning down at her, brow creased, worry lining his face.

Rachel's words cut into her thoughts. "Throughout the meal, he kept touching the pad's screen, like he was doing research or something. Eventually, he waved me down and asked for his check. He was smiling. I told him he looked like he'd just gotten some good news. He said he had, plopped a hundred-dollar bill on the table and told me to keep the change. On his way out, he said he was going to clean up a mess and he might even make some money while he was at it."

An audible sigh came through the phone. "Anyhow, something told me if that really was you in the picture, I should at least try to make contact."

"Thank you." She put a hand under

Apollo's chin and scratched his throat. "I can't tell you how much I appreciate it. I…" She hesitated. Could she trust Rachel?

She had no choice. "Please don't tell Peter you talked to me. I stumbled on something last Thursday night and he has sent people to kill me twice."

Rachel gasped. "Oh, my. He always seems so…nice."

"I thought so, too. But I'm begging you, don't let him know you talked to me. If he thinks he can use you to get to me, neither of us will be safe."

"I promise I won't say a thing."

"Thank you." She disconnected the call and rose.

Spence was still frowning. "That didn't look like good news."

"No." She stalked across the living room and back again while Spence waited. "That was a girl I worked with."

"I thought you said no one knew how to find you."

She heaved a sigh "When I said no one

knew my real name, I was wrong. The lady who just called—Rachel—we both worked at La Maison. We also worked together for a short time when I first landed in Atlanta, so she knew me before I had my name changed. Almost seven years later, she actually remembered Ashbaugh."

Alyssa relayed everything Rachel had told her. "She said she just got a quick glance, so it's possible it wasn't even me in the picture."

"Did she describe the photo?"

"Three people and a dog, and it looked like me in the middle."

Spence's frown deepened. "That sounds a lot like the photo Brandi took. When we get back to the apartment, how about if you email it to me from your phone, and I'll pull it up on my computer where we can enlarge it. Even if it's the same picture, there may not be anything that would identify where you were."

"That sounds good."

She walked back to the dining room,

still holding Kassie's phone. If there was no location metadata embedded in the photo and no places tagged in the post, even if Peter had the photo, it wouldn't do him any good.

But based on the comment he'd made when leaving La Maison, that *wasn't* the case. He'd apparently had a breakthrough, and she was sure it had something to do with the picture.

The best she could hope for was that Rachel was mistaken, that Peter and his minions hadn't seen the post and someone else was the subject of the photo he'd been studying.

If she was wrong, she was in deep trouble. Peter had put a tracking device on her car. He'd paid to have the mechanic work done so she wouldn't abandon it, and he'd sent someone to shoot at her. When that hadn't worked, he'd managed to obtain something lethal and have someone try to inject her with it. Those weren't the deeds of a man who gave up easily.

But if Peter really *did* have nothing more to go on than that Alyssa Anderson might have fled to somewhere near Tallahassee, she might have a chance of making it through this latest mess-up alive.

She would hold on to that hope until she learned otherwise.

Spence walked with Alyssa to the back door of what would eventually be his music store, Apollo trotting ahead of them.

The evening had started out great. Meeting Jared and getting reacquainted with Tony had been good. Letting the two men in on the situation with Alyssa had felt like shifting part of a heavy burden to someone else's shoulders.

Jared having a friend working with the Atlanta PD had put both his and Alyssa's minds at ease. After what she had been through, she wasn't likely to trust anybody. Spence understood her concerns. Men like Peter often had connections in law enforcement.

He unlocked the back door and turned on the hall light. "How about coming upstairs? I've at least got it furnished with a couch and a comfy chair."

"Sure."

During the short trip from Kassie's to the building downtown, she had emailed the photo Brandi had texted. Internet installation was on the schedule for next week. Tonight, he would use his mobile hotspot, as he'd been doing since he'd arrived.

He led Alyssa up the stairs and into the large room. The living area and kitchen were open. A door at the end of the counter led to a bedroom and adjoining bath.

Alyssa stepped into the space and looked around. "Would you believe, I've never been up here? When I was a kid, this was always rented." She smiled at him. "Your space is a lot better than mine."

"I'm afraid yours never got turned into living quarters."

"It's all right. It beats trying to live with either of my sisters."

"Hey, tonight went well."

"I guess it did, except for my little exchange with Kris."

"Not to take sides or anything, but I think she really *was* looking at you with concern instead of judgment."

Alyssa frowned. "Maybe I overreacted. I'm so used to them thinking the worst of me that I probably read it into everything they do. I'll try to work on that, especially if I'm going to be stuck here for a while."

He waved a hand toward the couch. "Have a seat, and I'll pull up your email."

By the time he had retrieved his computer from the bar in the kitchen area, Apollo had jumped up next to Alyssa on the couch and had his head resting in her lap.

"Okay, stinker. We're going to have a hard time looking at this together with a seventy-five-pound dog between us." He extended an index finger and pointed at the floor. "Down."

The dog obeyed, but there was a lot of reluctance in the motion.

Once Spence had positioned himself next to Alyssa, he patted the couch on his other side. "Come." The dog curled up beside him, head resting between his front paws.

"Now, for this picture." He turned on his phone's hotspot, opened his laptop and navigated to his email. Hers was right on top. After a couple of clicks, the picture filled the screen.

Alyssa leaned against him, studying what was there. Apollo's face filled the lower portion of the photo. Spence was squatting on one side of the dog, Brandi on the other, with Alyssa peering around her, putting her face between them. The Girl Scout table was behind them, colorful boxes stacked on top. Behind that was a blank wall.

A soft sigh escaped Alyssa as she

seemed to relax beside him. "There's no way to know where we are from this, no signage or anything."

He leaned closer, squinting at the screen. The right-hand portion of the Girl Scout banner was visible next to Brandi, its message too small to read.

He clicked to zoom in, expanding the photo to a hundred and twenty-five percent, then one-fifty, and all the way to two hundred. His chest tightened. The two lines of block characters were blurred but decipherable. The first was "OOP" with "15" below.

"Oh, no." Alyssa whispered the words beside him.

Spence opened a new tab and did a search for "Girl Scout Troop 115." North Carolina Coastal Pines 1 came up. Troop 215 was based in Carmel, Indiana. Troop 315 in Gainesville, Florida, a considerable distance from Pensacola.

A few more searches and he landed on Troop 715, Pensacola, Florida.

Alyssa stiffened. "If Peter saw this and blew it up like you just did, it wouldn't take him more than a few minutes to have a whole list of locations to check. Since he knows I'm from somewhere in Florida, my guess is he'll start here, maybe Gainesville first. Eventually, though, he's going to land in Pensacola."

She looked at him with wide, fear-filled eyes. "I've got to get out of here."

"When you're gone, do you really think he's going to stop looking for you?"

"Probably not. But wherever I go, there won't be a trail leading him to me."

"Maybe, but you don't know that. From what you've told me, this Peter sounds pretty resourceful. Let's see what the Atlanta police can do. In the meantime, let your family and me protect you."

A long span of silence passed before she finally nodded. "All right. But the first hint I get that Peter is anywhere in the vicinity, I'm out of here."

"Fair enough."

She reached both hands forward in a stretch. "If you don't mind walking me home, I'm going to try to get some sleep."

Apollo lifted his head, suddenly perking up. Whether he'd picked up on the word *walk* or *sleep*, Spence wasn't sure. Both were favorite activities. The dog often amazed him with how much he seemed to understand.

"Yep, come on. We're going to walk Alyssa home."

Apollo jumped down from the couch, looking from one to the other, tail wagging. As soon as they headed toward the open door leading downstairs, the dog charged ahead of them, his fast, heavy tread echoing in the narrow stairwell.

When Alyssa got to the lobby, she turned to face Spence. "This is a pain when I could just cut across the balcony to get from your place to mine. But no way am I going to leave my alarm off."

"I don't mind going the long way around. And *he* definitely doesn't." He nodded at his dog, who currently stood at the front door, tail wagging so furiously his whole rear end swayed back and forth. "I do have an idea, though. What if we remove the sensors from your balcony doors and install a separate single-zone system. Then you could arm and disarm it without leaving the second floor."

She nodded. "I like that idea. It just doesn't make sense for me to pay a security company to come out and install a new system when my stay here is temporary."

"It would be overkill. I'm guessing we could pick up something at Lowe's for less than a hundred bucks and I could install it for you." He'd always been pretty handy. If something came with DIY instructions, he could usually manage it.

When they stepped onto the sidewalk to head to the charter office entrance, Alyssa pulled the key from her pocket. "If you let me pay for the system, I'll accept your donation of time to install it."

The moment she opened the door, a steady high-pitched tone said the system was armed. She punched four numbers into the control panel and turned to him.

"Thank you. I can't tell you how much I appreciate everything you're doing for me. Eventually, this will be over and we'll both have our lives back."

Spence frowned. If getting his life back meant Alyssa wouldn't be in it, he wasn't so sure he wanted it back. He was getting used to having her around. They would never return to where they'd been before he'd left eight years ago, but he was developing high hopes for a lifelong friendship.

"If you need anything, call me. I want to hear from you if you feel at all scared or threatened." He smiled. "If you beat on the wall dividing our two units, I'd definitely wake up, even out of a sound sleep." Although he hadn't classified his sleep as "sound" for a while.

He wished her good-night and then watched her lock the door and rearm the alarm. "Okay, boy. One more opportunity to take care of business, and then it's bedtime."

Five minutes later, he climbed the stairs to his own apartment. He really needed to get some rest. But that wasn't likely to happen anytime soon, no matter how hard he tried.

Getting to sleep had been difficult for quite some time. Even when the nightmares didn't come, he was plagued with an ever-present tension, as if danger was around every corner, lurking in unseen places, waiting for him to let down his guard.

Now that situation was compounded times ten. Because he didn't just have to fear the demons that took up residence in his mind. There was also the very real threat to Alyssa. He'd feel better if he was sleeping on the charter office couch, downstairs from her.

God, please protect her, especially when I'm not there to do it.

He picked up his guitar and sat in the chair. Apollo stretched out on the couch adjacent to him, and Spence strummed a C chord, keeping the volume low enough to not disturb the other occupant of the building. Then he stopped to listen.

Silence, except for the lingering tones of what he'd just played.

Both the charter office and Alyssa's apartment above were protected by the security system. Besides that, she had promised to call him at the first sign of danger. He pulled his phone from his pocket and laid it on the arm of the chair.

Then he closed his eyes and breathed another prayer for her protection. He transitioned from C to A minor, consciously slowing his breathing. Then he picked up his phone to make sure he hadn't accidentally silenced the ringer. Hand once again on his guitar, he moved to F and finally G before repeating the four-chord pattern. It was a common progression, one he could play with no thought.

Ten minutes later, he wasn't any closer to sleep than when he'd started. He heaved a sigh. He was fighting a losing battle. He would never be able to totally relax.

Not as long as there were men out there determined to see Alyssa dead.

SEVEN

Spence bolted upright in bed, heart pounding out a frenzied rhythm, breath coming in jerky gasps.

He pressed one hand to his chest, the other to his cheek, wet from where Apollo had licked him.

As his breathing slowed, he lowered his hands to cup his dog's cheeks. "Thanks, buddy."

Only two days had passed since his last nightmare. That one had come Thursday night. He'd chalked it up to the disconcerting discovery that the picture Brandi had posted could lead Peter to Pensacola.

The nightmares always started the same, with him riding in a convoy, sometimes part of a route clearance team, sometimes coming through right behind them. Often-times the dreams played out exactly the same way the events had in real life. Other times, his mind chose alternate scenarios just as terrifying as the real thing.

The latter was the case with the dream he'd just had. Instead of McCarthy lying in the dusty road with useless legs and bullets whizzing past, it had been Alyssa. Before he could get her behind the berm, a man had appeared standing over them, an AK-47 aimed at Alyssa's head. Though Spence had never seen him before, he'd somehow known he was looking at Peter.

He pressed both hands to the top of his head and then slid them down his moist face. That wasn't just dog slobber. It was sweat.

He looked at the clock: 12:42. He still had another six or seven hours until he needed to be up. Sleep would come even-tually, but not anytime soon.

When he tugged on the sheet to throw it back, Apollo jumped from the bed.

The dog was used to Spence's routine on nights like this—sleep, wake up in a state of panic, get out of bed and go play for a while. And on the really good nights, actually get a few more hours of sleep.

On his way to the living room, he stopped at the kitchen for a bottle of water. That was part of the routine, too, not that it aided in sleep, but the panting and sweating usually left him thirsty.

He picked up his guitar and sank into the upholstered chair. Apollo took up his usual spot on the couch.

He strummed a G chord and began to sing softly. "Alleluia, alleluia…" It was an old worship chorus he rarely heard anymore, but he liked it and often played it during those lonely hours in the middle of the night.

There were other verses, things like "Thank you, Jesus" and "You are worthy." He often made up his own, each of them cries from the heart: "God, I need you," "Help me, Jesus" and "Lord, I trust you."

Any phrase worked, as long as it had four syllables and could be sung over and over.

When he finished, the last strains faded and other music came through the open door of his bedroom. His phone's ringtone. Who would be calling him at this hour?

He laid the guitar aside and reached the open doorway as the music died. When he checked his call log, Alyssa's name was on top. There would be only one reason for her call at this hour—some kind of threat.

He called her back with shaking hands. While waiting for her to pick up, he hurried onto his balcony. Nothing was amiss in front. The alarm next door wasn't going off, either.

After a click and soft rustle, her voice came through the phone. "Hey."

It was just a single word, but it didn't hold any fear or anxiety. His breath released in a rush. "Is everything okay?"

"Everything's fine. I heard you playing, so I thought—"

"You heard me?" *No way.* Annoyance

wove through him. If he couldn't even play softly to soothe himself when sleep eluded him, these living arrangements were going to be tough. "Do you have supersonic hearing or something?"

She laughed. "Actually, I put my ear to the wall to see if you were awake. I didn't want to call you if you were asleep." She paused. "Can I come over?"

The irritation he'd felt moments earlier evaporated in an instant. "Sure. I'll meet you on the balcony."

Yesterday, they'd purchased a security system from Lowe's, like they'd talked about Thursday night. Today, he'd gotten it installed. Now that going from one apartment to the other involved just a short walk across the balcony, something told him these middle-of-the-night visits might become a regular thing. He was all right with that.

As he stepped onto the balcony, one of the French doors at the other end swung

open and Alyssa stepped out. The bath-
robe she wore fell almost to her ankles.

He smiled as she approached.

"No Bugs Bunny tonight?"

"Oh, Bugs Bunny is here. I've just got
him covered up. It's chilly tonight."

She was right. By mid-September, night-
time temperatures could get a little nippy.

He led her into the apartment and motioned toward the couch. "Have a seat. Can
I get you anything?"

"No, I'm good."

"Are you sure? I have one Caramel
Chocolate Chip Cookie left. I'll split it
with you."

"You did good. My Thin Mints were
gone two days ago."

"I polished off at least a quarter of them."

"That's right. So I'll take you up on your
offer to split the last cookie."

As soon as she sat, Apollo jumped up
next to her. When Spence returned with
the cookie, he sat in the chair he had va-

cated a few minutes earlier rather than fight with his dog. "How was dinner?"

He'd walked over to the charter office at lunchtime and talked to Alyssa and Kris. Kassie had been taking care of appointments at her hair salon. Kris had told him Jared was working tonight and Tony had a meeting, so the three girls had decided to make dinner in the charter office kitchen and eat together, along with Gavin. Kris had invited Spence to join them, but he'd passed, refusing to intrude on their sister time.

Alyssa smiled. "Actually, it was really nice."

"No friction?"

"Not a bit, even with the three of us bumping into each other in that tiny kitchen. I'm still not holding my breath, but tonight was good. Kris brought a couple of bags of clothes from home, stuff she said she was planning to donate and thought she'd let me go through it first."

She gave him a wry smile. "I know I'm

not in a position to be picky, but I have to say every item in there was something that fit me and was a style I'd wear. That tells me when Kris went through her closet, it had less to do with a desire to declutter and more to do with wanting to help a needy sister. But this was how she could do it and not make me feel like a charity case." She frowned. "Even though I sort of am right now."

"Only because you had to leave everything behind when you made your quick getaway."

"You make it sound much more palatable." She pressed her lips together. "Did you know they still do Gallery Night here? Kassie mentioned it at dinner. It's next Friday, and Jared and Justice are going to be working it, doing patrol."

He crossed his arms. "Don't even think about it. You three ladies cooked and ate at the charter office to keep you out of public."

"I know. It's just really appealing. If I

have to stay cooped up inside for much longer, I'm afraid I'm going to go stir crazy."

"It's just temporary. Once you know you're safe, you can do all the Gallery Nights you want to."

He remembered the event well. The third Friday of every month, thousands would converge on downtown Pensacola for a time of music, art and food. He and Alyssa had gone several times and always enjoyed it. The streets had been packed, the air filled with fun and excitement.

That was then. Now crowds triggered panic attacks. Thankfully, that was something he wouldn't have to face, at least not in the near future. Until Peter and all his cronies were behind bars, being out in public was something Alyssa couldn't even consider.

She leaned against the arm of the couch and curled her legs up, tucking her sock-clad feet in next to her. Apollo moved over to accommodate her. "When I called, you were playing. I'd love it if you would continue."

"Sure." He picked up his guitar and placed it across his lap. After strumming some random chords, he settled on one of the songs he and the worship team had done the last Sunday before leaving La-Grange.

As he played, Alyssa propped her right elbow on the arm of the couch and rested the side of her head in her hand. Her features settled into an expression of contentment.

As long as he'd known her, she had never played or sung. Kassie had been the musical one of the Ashbaugh girls. But Alyssa had always enjoyed listening to him play, something that apparently hadn't changed.

When he finished, she lifted her head. "That doesn't sound like one of our old rock-and-roll songs."

"Nope, I haven't played those in quite a while." Eight years, to be exact. "Most of what I play now are songs I know from church."

"Wait." She sat straighter. "What?"

"Yep. For the past three months, I've played on my church's worship team." That had started shortly after he'd gotten Apollo. As venturing from his apartment had gradually grown easier, he'd transitioned from watching the service online to attending in person, which had rapidly led to helping with the music.

She swung her feet onto the floor. "You play in a worship band? At church?"

"I did until a week ago. I'm going to your sisters' church tomorrow. If they need any help, I'll volunteer."

Alyssa shook her head. "I'm still trying to imagine you *attending church,* let alone being involved. Tell me how that happened."

"I kind of took the roundabout way, but I guess you'd say it started with Steve's overdose."

It had been almost eight years, and the

scene still haunted him. The band had finished practicing and had begun partying. They'd all been at Steve's house. Since he was the one with the large garage, practices—and parties—had always been held there.

Spence shook his head. "We had big dreams, the four of us—Braydon, Bryson, Steve and me. We all thought we were destined for fame and glory, looking forward to lives of glitz and glamour, listening to the screams of adoring fans. But no matter how you pitch it, there's nothing glamorous about dying in one's vomit."

Alyssa winced. Although she'd been with him at almost every party he'd attended from age sixteen to eighteen, that night she'd been at home sick with the flu. It had turned out to be a blessing in disguise.

"What I saw shook me to the core. It was enough to scare me straight. But it wasn't until I was in Afghanistan, pinned down by enemy fire, that I cried out to

God. Some people say you're not supposed to bargain with God. I'd say if you do, make sure you're ready to come through on whatever you promise. I told God if He would save me, I'd commit the rest of my life to Him. God did, and I honored the promise I'd made."

He strummed a chord and then flattened his hand across the strings. "I hope you'll go to church with me sometime soon."

She frowned. "You're not going to get me into church, especially with my sisters. They're always trying to fix me, and I don't need fixing." She gave him a half smile. "Well, maybe I do, but definitely not by them. I'll fix myself."

"We can't fix ourselves. It took me going halfway around the world to find that out."

"Whatever." She settled back into the position she'd been in earlier, legs curled up, elbow propped on the arm of the couch. Apollo rested his head on her feet. "Don't hold out hope for getting me into church, but you can play for me anytime. I won't even object to your singing those songs."

Those songs would be worship songs. Since she'd given him free rein to sing whatever he wanted, that was what she would get. Sometimes music had a way of touching hearts when sermons couldn't.

After thinking for a moment, he played the intro for "Graves Into Gardens." Every time he sang the song, he felt as if the lyrics had been written for him. He really had searched the world over and hadn't found anything that satisfied. Not until one afternoon along a dusty road in Afghanistan. When all was said and done, he'd had to agree: There really was nothing better than Jesus.

When finished, he made a smooth transition into "I Speak Jesus." Another song with lyrics he hoped would touch Alyssa. What struggles did she face that needed the Savior's touch? Did she have dark addictions to break? What about fear, anxiety and depression? She definitely needed hope and freedom and peace. He didn't even have to ask that.

As he continued to play and sing, Alyssa slid further down the couch, nudging Apollo out of the way until her head rested on the padded arm. Her eyelids grew gradually heavier and then closed altogether.

And he continued to play, softly, so he wouldn't disturb her. Her mouth was closed, her lips curved up ever so slightly, as if she'd found the peace in sleep that always eluded her when she was awake.

God, please let me have a positive impact on her. Turn her heart toward You.

How different would their lives have been if he had chosen more constructive outlets for dealing with his abusive father, if he'd led Alyssa to church instead of down a path of self-destruction?

They'd probably be married by now, with a couple of kids. Instead, Alyssa still hadn't forgiven him for leaving her and couldn't wait to get out of town. And they both had enough baggage to fill the back of a semitrailer.

He transitioned into another song, Chris McClarney's "Beauty for Ashes." The opening referred to God as a God of new beginnings.

Spence was still waiting for some of the ashes in his life to be turned to beauty.

But he'd found his new beginning.

God, please let Alyssa find hers.

People packed Palafox Street. The crowd was energized, an atmosphere of celebration in the air. Galleries lined both sides of the street, interspersed with restaurants and bars. All establishments were open, inviting guests to view the variety of artwork displayed or to come in for a meal or drink.

Alyssa had almost resigned herself to hanging out on the balcony and looking down Government Street toward Palafox, hoping to catch a glimpse of the goings-on a couple of blocks away.

This was a whole lot better.

She looked over her shoulder at Spence, standing at the edge of the sidewalk, right behind her. Apollo stood beside him in his black vest. Kassie and Kris were to her right, with Tony between them. Jared was somewhere in the crowd. He'd promised to do his best to keep checking on them, but he had a job to do.

Last Saturday night, she'd fallen asleep on Spence's couch and hadn't awoken until three in the morning. During those two hours, she'd slept harder than she had in…she couldn't remember when she'd last slept that soundly. The sense of security knowing Spence was so close and the comfort of Apollo lying on the couch with her, head resting on her feet, had put her in a state of relaxed oblivion.

For the past week, she'd been a mess. Jared had contacted his buddy in Atlanta the day after the cookout at Kassie's. For the next three days, she'd worried that the information on her whereabouts had somehow found its way back to Peter.

More than a week had passed since her conversation with Rachel. The first one anyway. There'd been two since, both initiated by Alyssa. As recently as last night, Peter had dined at La Maison. Whatever photo Rachel had seen on his tablet, he hadn't pulled it up since. At least, not at dinner. She'd been watching, even going so far as to make sure she was his server. She'd been employed there long enough to make those kinds of demands, regardless of how much the other servers wanted his generous gratuities.

Besides the fact that Peter hadn't left Atlanta, there'd been no other signs of anyone looking for her. She'd gradually gone from jittery, expecting Peter to materialize in the charter office lobby, to having such bad cabin fever she was going to hurt someone if she couldn't get outside those four walls.

Having her stitches removed on Monday hadn't even offered a means of escape. When she'd mentioned to Kris that she needed a ride to the walk-in clinic, Kris had volunteered Mildred. She wasn't just Gavin's babysitter. She was a retired nurse. She'd been happy to come to the office with her scissors and tweezers and go to work.

This afternoon, Alyssa had finally demanded to know how long everyone expected her to stay cooped up when there wasn't the slightest hint that Peter even knew where she was. It had taken a lot of convincing, but she'd finally gotten her sisters, both of their fiancés and Spence to agree to let her go out for just an hour, under their watchful eyes, of course. She even felt somewhat disguised, with her hair twisted into a bun beneath an Atlanta Braves baseball cap.

She glanced over her shoulder again, ready to give Spence an appreciative smile. He'd been the most reluctant to acquiesce to her wishes.

Spence wasn't looking at her, though. He was standing straight and stiff, head pivoting from side to side, gaze darting erratically over the crowd. He was tense, hypervigilant. Had he seen something? Danger? Some kind of threat?

"Spence?" She raised her voice over the conversations going on around her and the music pouring from the stage set up a short distance away. He didn't acknowledge her.

She called his name even louder, and when that didn't work, she grasped his shoulder and gave him a small shake. His eyes met hers. They seemed to hold a wildness she'd never seen before.

"Hey, it's okay. Tony and my sisters are right here. Jared's somewhere nearby, too, with Justice. Nothing's going to happen."

He nodded, but the motion was jerky. She grasped his hand. "Come on, let's get a little closer to the band."

She wove through the crowd, pulling him along behind her. Immersing himself in the songs would be good for him. Music had always had the ability to pull him out of whatever funk he was in.

She moved closer, Spence's hand in hers, until they were only about ten feet from the front of the stage. The group, likely composed of local musicians, was performing songs from eras spanning the '70s to present day. She didn't know them, but they were good.

As the current song drew to a close, the crowd erupted into applause with lots of whoops and hollers.

Alyssa turned to smile at Spence. "Isn't this bet—" She swallowed the rest of the word.

In the glow of the streetlights, sweat glistened on his forehead and the sides of his face. His jaw was clenched, and the wildness she'd seen in his eyes earlier was still there, times ten. Apollo was pressed against his leg, but he seemed unaware of the dog.

Realization slammed into her. Spence

was on the verge of a panic attack, and it had nothing to do with her.

She leaned close to him. "Let's get out of here."

Spence didn't move. She gave him a small shove. "Come on, let's go home."

He gave her another one of those jerky nods and then grasped her hand and spun. Behind them, the band began its next song. As Spence made his way through the crowd, her hand in his, Apollo's leash in the other, his pace grew faster and more frenzied. Soon he was bumping people out of the way without so much as an "excuse me." In their mad dash, she'd lost Tony and her sisters. Maybe they'd gotten separated when she'd dragged Tony toward the stage.

Just before they reached the edge of the street, a man crowded between them from her right. He was Spence's height, but outweighed him by a good forty pounds. A second pressed in from the left. She glanced from one to the other. Neither of them was looking at her. Were they even aware they had worked their way between her and Spence?

The music behind them swelled, growing more driving, and the crowd roared. The men slowed their pace, holding her back. Her hand slipped through Spence's. A moment later, she lost sight of him.

"Spence!" Even as she shouted his name, she knew it was pointless. He would never hear her over the music and the noise of the crowd.

One man stayed on her right as the other circled behind her. Soon, she was being jostled to the left, farther and farther away from Spence and Apollo. Yes, the men knew exactly what they were doing. Within seconds, they had pressed her out of the crowd and were forcing her toward an alley between two buildings. Parked cars lined one side. No one was milling around any of them.

When she twisted to make her way back into the safety of the crowd, the man next to her grasped her upper arm in a vise-like grip. She released a loud scream. A meaty hand clamped over her mouth, immediately cutting it off. The same man wrapped his other arm around her waist, and her feet left the ground.

Panic pounded up her spine. She clawed at the hand covering her mouth and kicked the man's shins. Her feeble attempts did nothing but make him angry. He tightened his hold and gave her a rough shake.

He had carried her past the first parked car. Within moments, they would be too far away for anyone to help her. They probably already were.

As she twisted and fought, she forced her mouth open beneath the man's hand. Once she had pulled her lips back, she clamped down hard on the meaty flesh of his palm.

He released a high-pitched scream that dissolved into a string of curses. The bite had accomplished what she had hoped. The man still held her, but he had removed his hand, which was likely now bleeding. She twisted her head back and forth, shrieking Spence's name, then Apollo's, and then general cries for help.

"Shut up!"

The man dropped her, but the other one grabbed her before she could even think about running away. Now they had passed the second car, leaving Palafox Street even farther behind.

A bark sounded somewhere behind them, muffled by the noise still pouring from the street. The man who held her spun suddenly, swinging her around with him. A chocolate Lab was bounding toward them.

Apollo?

Before she had a chance to ponder it further, another dog raced into the alley, a German shepherd. Both dogs wore working vests. The man who held her released her. The other one had already made it to the opposite end of the alley and was rounding the back corner of the building.

When she landed, her knees buckled.

As she crumpled to the ground, a uniformed police officer charged into the alley, weapon drawn. Recognition dawned as pain shot through her right knee. *Not again.*

Jared was some distance back when Apollo reached her. The Lab released a couple of whimpers and then ran his wet tongue up one cheek. She wrapped her arms around him as Justice raced past, gaze focused intently ahead. The German shepherd went airborne, clamping his jaws around the elbow of the man who had just held her. He released a scream and dropped to his knees. Justice held on. The dog probably wouldn't release him until commanded by his partner to do so.

Jared slowed. "Are you okay?"

"I'm fine. Go see to him. There's another man, too. He ran behind the building—that way." She held up one arm.

Jared jogged away from her, talking into his radio as he did. Then he gave Justice the command to release. The dog sat, tense and ready to react as Jared handcuffed the suspect.

One man dead, one soon to be behind bars. How many more were there? Eventually the authorities would work their way up to Peter and his cronies. Only then would she be safe.

She looked back at Palafox Street. Why wasn't Apollo with Spence? "Where is your daddy?"

As if in answer to her question, Spence hurried into the alley, his limp more pronounced than usual. He rushed toward her and dropped to his knees beside her. "I'm so sorry. I let you down. I'm so sorry."

The grief in his voice broke her heart. She cupped his cheeks in both hands. "Hey, it wasn't your fault. Those two guys were bigger than you. And they were *way* bigger than me. They were able to separate us, and there's nothing you could have done differently."

Two more police officers rushed into the

alley. One hurried to assist Jared, and the other stopped next to her and Spence.

"Braydon?" They both said his name together.

"In the flesh. Brandi told me she ran into you guys." He slipped right back into professional mode. "Can you describe the other man who attacked you?"

"Caucasian, maybe thirties or forties. It's hard to say because he was bald. Probably six feet. A big guy, muscular."

"Facial hair?"

"A close-cut beard and mustache."

"Clothing?"

"Jeans and a gray hoodie."

Braydon radioed her description to Dispatch and once again addressed her. "They're putting out a BOLO."

"Thank you." She looked at Spence. "I could try to convince myself this was random, but I like to think I'm smarter than that. Peter has managed to track me to Pensacola, and I'm not going to try to convince myself otherwise."

When she attempted to push herself to her feet, Spence rose and held out a hand. She accepted the assistance. The knee was tender, but not much more than it had been earlier tonight. Maybe she'd just irritated it rather than really set herself back.

She started to offer another thank you, but when she looked at him, what she saw drew her up short.

He faced Palafox, where light drifted into the alley and illuminated his face. He looked rough. Though the wildness had left his eyes, his face was several shades of pale, lines of fatigue embedded in his features.

She'd thought Apollo's service was for physical reasons; Spence had obviously been injured. Maybe she was right. Maybe Apollo *did* give him physical assistance.

But that wasn't all. Apollo was there for emotional support. Whatever experiences Spence had had while fighting on the other side of the world, they had left him with emotional trauma. Maybe even PTSD. And that was why he had Apollo.

The realization left her with a hollowness deep in her gut. Spence hadn't wanted to come tonight, and she had pushed him into it. Her sole focus had been on how tired she was of being trapped inside those four walls and how badly she'd wanted to get out, without a single thought for how the event might affect Spence. Maybe her sisters had been right all along. Maybe she *was* selfish.

She didn't deserve the care and concern Spence was showing her, the way he had taken on her problems when he clearly had enough of his own.

This was just one more reason she needed to leave. At this point, Spence might not even try to stop her.

Because, after the events of this evening, he would probably be glad to see her go.

EIGHT

Spence walked down the sidewalk bordering East Government Street, the noise of the festivities growing gradually more distant. Alyssa was next to him, Jared and Justice to their rear. The law enforcement team was providing an escort all the way to the charter office. When they'd left the alley, they'd run into Kassie, Kris and Tony, and Alyssa had given them a brief rundown of the attack. Her account had almost made it sound like he hadn't messed up.

Now, Apollo was at his side. In fact, if the dog was any closer, they'd be tripping over each other's feet. Once making sure Alyssa was all right, Apollo had pretty much stayed glued to his hip. The

Lab instinctively knew when he wasn't doing well.

This was one of those times. Usually, when he had his incidents, he was alone. Even when he was in public, it never affected anyone else. Tonight it had. He'd almost enabled Alyssa's abduction.

When he and Alyssa had reached Palafox Street and he'd seen the crowds, it had started almost immediately—the anxiety, the hypervigilance, the sense danger was all around them. He'd fought to beat back the panic, using every rational argument he could come up with, and Apollo had done everything he'd been trained to do.

By the time Alyssa had suggested going home, Spence had been at the breaking point. He'd grabbed her hand and turned, ready to make his way back through the crowd. Soon he hadn't been aware of anything except getting away and retreating into the safety of his apartment. At some point, he'd lost his grip on Alyssa's hand.

He couldn't even say when that had happened.

But as he'd headed down the sidewalk toward Government Street, Apollo had begun to tug at the leash, trying to pull him in the opposite direction. That had been when he'd realized he'd lost Alyssa.

What a loser. He wasn't only unfit for military duty. He couldn't even protect the woman he… What? Cared for. They had ended their relationship, but he had never stopped caring for her. No matter what happened, she would always hold a special place in his heart.

When they arrived at the charter office, Alyssa slipped her key into the lock. Once inside, she disarmed the alarm system and turned to face him.

"I'm sorry."

He looked at her. "For what? I'm the one who should be apologizing." Of course, he already had.

"I should never have insisted on going out tonight."

He shrugged. "Hindsight's always twenty-twenty. You had no idea you were going to be attacked in the midst of hundreds of people."

She frowned. "Yeah, going out was a mistake in that sense. But that wasn't what I was referring to. You were opposed right from the start. I thought it was just concern for my safety."

"That was a lot of it."

"But there was more. I should have seen that."

"How? It isn't like I've given you much to go on." He hadn't told her anything about the past eight years, other than that he'd gotten out of the army and had been living in LaGrange for the past year.

Could he share his struggles with her? He hadn't shared the details of the horrors he'd experienced—or the psychological and emotional fallout from them—with anyone except the veterans in the Sierra Delta community. But Alyssa had plenty of her own issues. If there was anyone outside of other veterans he should feel comfortable sharing his troubles with, it should be her.

After a few more moments of hesitation, he twisted the dead bolt into the locked position. "How about rearming this and coming up to my place?"

"Sure."

She led him up the stairs. After disarming and rearming the system he had installed, she secured the French doors, and they walked across the balcony to his quarters. When he unlocked and swung open the door, there was no alarm system to worry about. The security company had come out on Wednesday. They'd quoted him a combination price for both installation and monitoring that had included a sizable discount. So he'd ordered the system and signed a two-year monitoring agreement.

Soon, he would have a lot of expensive sound and musical equipment downstairs. In the event someone broke in, he'd wanted the security of knowing the police would be there within minutes to protect his merchandise.

Alyssa sat on the couch, and he took a seat next to her. Apollo hopped up on his other side and laid his head in his lap. The dog sensed he was still needed. Although Spence was doing much better than he had been fifteen minutes ago, the experience had left him with a jittery weakness in his limbs that still hadn't fully dissipated.

He took a deep breath, not sure where to begin, then decided it didn't matter where he started, as long as he got the story out.

"During my time over there, I saw a lot of death and destruction. Not just random, either. These were buddies—guys whose stories I knew, men who had shared their dreams and plans for the future, brothers."

He stroked Apollo's head as he talked, smoothing the fur between his eyes, over the top of his head and down his neck, then back to the top to do it again.

"There was also the constant state of

being on edge—the mortar fire that would have us flying out of bed in the middle of the night, the convoys down roads where Taliban could be hiding behind every rise or berm. That feeling of not knowing which of us wouldn't live to see another day."

Alyssa shook her head. "I can't even imagine."

"It took its toll. I thought once I came home, I'd be able to put it all behind me and return to a normal life. That didn't happen. All those experiences I'd thought I was leaving over there followed me home in my nightmares."

"How did you get Apollo?"

"I was dealing with a lot of depression, unable to sleep, spending my days vegging in front of the TV, taking a whole cocktail of medications just to try to make it through each day. I'd tried praying, but it seemed like those prayers weren't getting past the ceiling. I was getting counseling through the VA, and my counselor suggested putting in an application for a service dog through K9s For Warriors."

He slid his hand farther down Apollo's back, and the dog released a sigh. "I didn't want to do it. I was afraid I'd be taking a dog away from a veteran who might need it worse than I did. During one session, my counselor got online and made me start the application process right then and there."

He smiled. Starting that application was one of the best decisions he'd ever made, even though he'd had to be prodded into making it.

"I take it getting Apollo helped."

"It did, more than you can imagine. I waited eight months, which is actually super fast. I think God moved some mountains."

"I'm not wishing sleep problems on you, but it's been kind of nice having company on those nights I was awake."

He grinned. "Glad I could accommodate you. It is getting better, though. The nightmares are a long way from gone, but they aren't as frequent as they used to be. Once I got Apollo, I felt like I might be able to start living again. That's when I started working on my dream to have a music store. I applied for a small business loan, and now here I am. I've still got a long way to go, but at least I'm moving in the right direction."

"I'm glad." She turned her head to look up at him, eyebrows drawn together. "You have a gun. I didn't think you were allowed to own one when you have PTSD." She had watched a movie a while back where a veteran had a flashback while at the shooting range and killed his buddy.

"Depends on the situation. I've never been a danger to myself or anyone else. I *am* smart enough to leave my pistol out of reach while I'm sleeping, though."

"What happened tonight? Did you see something or hear something?" She paused. "If you don't want to talk about it, I understand."

"It's okay. I don't mind." Now that he'd

gotten started, it wasn't as difficult as he'd thought it would be. "Large crowds are one of my triggers."

"Oh, man. I really feel bad."

He put an arm around her. "Don't. You had no way of knowing I was going to freak out."

She snuggled against him, resting her head just above his collarbone. He released a sigh. This was contentment—Alyssa nestled against one side, his dog on the other, big, furry head in his lap.

Ever since reconnecting with Alyssa, she'd regularly mentioned her plans to leave Pensacola as soon as she could, emphasizing that her stay was temporary. Each time, it had bothered him a little more than the last time. He'd blamed it on the sense of protectiveness he felt around her, the fact that if she left, he would no longer be there to protect her.

But it was more than that. She had changed since those early days. She was more settled, more mature. And though she was struggling, she was trying hard to make the right choices. He was really intrigued with the woman she had become.

Once Peter and his buddies were no longer a threat, would Spence be ready to let her go? Probably not. What about once her animosity toward him dissolved and they could part ways as friends, without any hard feelings? Probably not.

What if he could influence her to return to the faith of her childhood and find the healing he had found? If he knew she was finally in a right relationship with God, would he want to let her go then? No, he wouldn't.

The problem was, the more time he spent with her, the more he realized the feelings he'd had for her so long ago had never died. He'd carried them all the way to Afghanistan and then Kuwait. Then, instead of leaving them there on the other side of the world, he'd brought them right back home.

He clenched his jaw. He'd buried those

feelings before. He would bury them again. When she was once again safe, he would have to let her go. Growing up with an alcoholic father, a mother she'd thought had deserted her and a past filled with wrong choices, she needed someone stable, not someone whose background was as shaky as hers, who had made the same wrong choices and was currently plagued by flashbacks and nightmares.

God had put her in his path. He had no doubt. The reasons were pretty clear. He was to protect her the best he could, try to lead her into a relationship with Him and be a true friend. But not anything more.

A minute or so passed before Alyssa once again sat up straight. "Have you talked to your father since you left for the Middle East?"

"No. I did send him a postcard when I got home, letting him know I was out of the army and had made it back to the States alive. I never heard from him."

He'd written his return address on the

postcard before he'd sent it. He could have written his phone number on it but hadn't been able to bring himself to do it.

Alyssa nodded, lips pressed together. "I haven't talked to mine, either. Every time I think about what he did—killing Mom, even if it was an accident, and letting us three girls believe she'd abandoned us... If I had to talk to him, I don't think it would be pretty. I'm afraid I would hurt him."

"I would tell you that you need to let the bitterness go, that it's probably doing you more harm than it is him, but then I'd have to take my own advice."

She smiled. "It's annoying how that works, huh?" She grew serious again. "Kassie and Kris say they've both forgiven him. I guess they're better people than I am, because I don't think I'll ever get there."

"I will eventually." He would have to. Those verses in the Bible about forgiveness had been haunting him for a while, long before his accident and return to the

States. Especially disturbing were the ones that said if he didn't forgive others, God wouldn't forgive him. That was some serious stuff.

When he'd been on the other side of the world, it had been easy to put off what he'd known he would eventually have to do. After arriving in LaGrange, he'd been struggling with too many other issues to deal with that one. But since he'd returned to Pensacola, the still, small voice had been getting louder and more persistent. His argument that he needed to straighten his own life out first was getting weaker and weaker.

"I talk to my mom pretty regularly, though." During his deployments, he'd kept in touch through the mail. Since his discharge, those weekly letters had turned into weekly phone calls.

"Six months after I left, she walked out. Got tired of the abuse. She's now living near my grandparents in Texas."

"I'm glad she got out. No one deserves

that." She lifted a hand to cover a yawn. "I might actually be able to get to sleep tonight. I'm ready to give it a try if you'll walk me home."

He tensed at the thought of her alone in her apartment next door. "Do you think there's any chance Peter and his men know where you're staying?"

"I doubt it. If they did, they would have attacked me here rather than in the midst of hundreds of people. My guess is that Peter had Brandi's photo and analyzed it the same way we did. It wouldn't have taken them long to land in Pensacola."

Spence nodded. "And they came out on Gallery Night hoping they would run into you. Even though the likelihood was slim, it obviously paid off."

She frowned. "I'm afraid tonight was my last time escaping this building anytime in the near future."

At least they were in agreement on that. "You really don't want anyone knowing where you are, outside of your sisters and me, in case these guys ask around."

Of course, if they asked around, someone was likely to mention her given last name, which would lead them to the charter office. He needed to come up with a better way to protect her.

He rose from the couch and held out a hand to help her up.

As she rose, she winced.

His chest squeezed. "The men didn't hurt you, did they?"

"When they let go of me, I came down on my knee again. It's just a little stiff. I don't think I undid much of the progress I've made over the past two weeks."

They headed to the back door and then across the balcony, both their limps slightly more pronounced than before. Sitting always made him stiff, especially after a prolonged time of being up. Alyssa seemed to be having the same problem. They made quite the pair.

When she unlocked and opened the door,

a steady high-pitched tone said the system was still armed, proving no one could have gotten inside. She stepped into her apartment and, after punching in the four-digit code, turned to face him. "Thank you for sharing. It really means a lot."

"Thank you for listening." That had meant a lot, too. She had listened without judgment, had even seemed to empathize with him. She'd never seen combat, but she'd had plenty of trauma throughout her life. They probably had more in common, even as adults, than he realized.

When he returned to his own apartment, he headed toward his bedroom. Some of the fatigue Alyssa felt was quickly settling over him. After changing into a T-shirt and a pair of gym shorts, he climbed into bed. Apollo landed in the spot next to him with a *whoomp*.

An hour later, he got back up. Hopefully Alyssa had been more successful finding sleep than he had. He walked to the living room, headed for the chair and his guitar. Instead of jumping up on the couch, Apollo walked to the door at the top of the stairs and looked back at him, wagging his tail.

"Seriously? You want to go out now?"

Maybe the dog was bored. Or maybe he really had to go. Spence slipped his pistol into one pocket of his shorts and his phone and a small plastic bag into the other, and then headed for the stairs. Oh, well. It wasn't like the trip was cutting into his sleep.

After slipping outside and locking the back door, he headed into the night, away from the parking area. At this hour, no one was out and about. He'd checked before he'd even stepped fully from the building.

He led Apollo to a patch of grass a little farther down where the dog could do his business, if he really had any to do. After some serious sniffing, the Lab briefly lifted his leg against a shrub and then tugged at the leash to go home. Yep, that was more about boredom than a real need to go. The small plastic bag would return empty.

He shook his head and fell into step behind his dog. As he drew closer to the Ashbaugh building, his steps faltered. Someone was approaching the back of the charter office. Spence hurried silently forward, his pulse in high gear.

The figure ahead of him tried the doorknob. After stepping back, he suddenly raised and thrust his foot outward. The shrill squeal of the alarm spilled into the night. A second later, the man disappeared inside.

Spence pulled out his weapon and broke into a full run, ignoring the pain in his hip. Someone was inside with Alyssa. As he reached the open door, the figure left the hall and disappeared around the corner of the lobby, a silhouette against the glow of the streetlights coming in the front window.

Spence ran down the hall, bursting into

the lobby as the man opened the door leading to the stairs. He aimed his pistol.

"Don't move."

The man spun. Shock morphed to indecision in the glow of the streetlights. His right hand slowly moved toward the holster at his hip.

Spence's jaw tightened. "Bad choice. Both hands in the air now, or you'll share the fate of your buddy in the woods along 85."

After one more second of hesitation, the intruder slowly lifted his hands. Something dark smeared his right palm, possibly blood. If that was from a bite, Alyssa had gotten him good.

"Now, on the floor, face down."

When he had complied, Spence stepped closer. Apollo moved with him. The dog had stayed at his side from the moment Spence had stopped in the lobby.

While keeping the pistol aimed between the man's shoulder blades, he pulled his phone from his pocket with his left hand and dialed 911.

As he relayed everything to Dispatch, he cast repeated glances up the stairs. Where was Alyssa? There was no way the man could have already gotten to her. Maybe she was hiding. That would be smart.

Sirens sounded in the distance and grew closer. Soon, blue flashing lights strobed through the front window. Without taking his eyes, or his weapon, off the man on the floor, he sidestepped to the front door. Before unlocking it, he cast a glance through the small rectangular panes of glass to verify that a cop stood there.

It wasn't just any cop. It was Alyssa's future brother-in-law with his K9 partner. After a quick command for Apollo to sit, Spence unlocked the door and motioned Jared and Justice inside. While Jared cuffed the man on the floor, Spence explained what had happened.

Soon, soft footsteps sounded on the stairs, and Spence looked up to see Alyssa descending in her Bugs Bunny pajamas. Relief poured through him and, when she reached the bottom of the stairs, he had to restrain himself to keep from wrapping her in a hug.

He dipped his head at the man Jared had just pulled to his feet. "I had taken Apollo out and was getting back just as this guy kicked in your back door. I'll secure it the best I can tonight and then fix it properly tomorrow."

"I'm afraid you have another door to fix."

"I do?"

She gave him a sheepish smile, which looked more like a grimace. "As soon as the alarm sounded, I jumped from the bed to run over to your place. When I couldn't get you to the door, I kicked it in." She lifted her shoulders in a prolonged shrug. "Sorry."

Now he did give in to the urge to hug her, but settled for a casual sideways hug instead. "No problem. I'm sorry I wasn't there. You'll have to blame this guy. He convinced me he needed to go out."

As if sensing they were talking about him, Apollo rose and padded over to them, tail wagging. Alyssa bent to ruffle the fur on his neck and back.

Spence watched her with his dog, heart twisting.

Tomorrow he would fix the doors. But it wouldn't be good enough. Alyssa needed to be somewhere safe.

Wherever that was, he wasn't about to let her do it alone.

Alyssa sat at the desk in the Ashbaugh Charters lobby, staring at the computer monitor, one hand on the mouse, her stuffed backpack leaning against her chair.

It was nine in the morning. After the break-in at the charter office, she had slept on Spence's couch. He'd refused to leave her alone. She hadn't argued. Even with the temporary repairs he'd made to the back door and the alarm armed, the thought of staying there terrified her.

This morning when she'd awoken, everything had been so quiet in Spence's room that she'd slipped quietly out the balcony door and into her own place, not wanting to disturb him.

That had been forty minutes ago. Now she was showered, dressed, and her meager belongings packed, ready to once again take off. She'd made her decision last night.

The thought shredded her heart. Over the past two weeks, she'd struggled to keep the walls she had erected so long ago intact. But last night, as Spence had opened up to her, sharing his struggles, the last of those barriers had crumbled. Those moments of total honesty and shared trauma had forged a bond.

When she'd snuggled against him, everything had felt so right. Did they have any chance at all of reclaiming what they had once shared, before Spence had changed and she hadn't, before he'd taken off and she'd let resentment simmer for eight long years? If Peter was out of the picture and she was safe, would she have the courage to even try?

The answer was irrelevant, because Peter wasn't out of the picture and she wasn't safe. Not by a long shot.

She heaved a sigh and clicked inside the first of three boxes on the screen. She was on the Kayak site, looking for the best deals on airfare. So far, she hadn't seen anyone this morning. Neither Kassie nor Kris had arrived. Kris would likely be walking in the door any minute. Kassie had hair appointments at her salon this morning and would then be helping Buck with a charter this afternoon. Maybe she would drop by the office in between, maybe not.

If Spence knew what Alyssa was doing, he would try to talk her into staying. So would her sisters. But she couldn't do it.

She couldn't stay and be a sitting duck for Peter and his goons.

She typed "PNS" into the from field and hovered over the next box. She'd begun her time at the computer with putting "Cities with good public transportation" into a Google search. She'd eliminated Portland, Seattle, Boston, Chicago and four others as being too cold. She was a Florida girl. Atlanta was about as cold as she wanted to get.

That had left only San Francisco, at least on the first search. She filled it into the second box and changed "round trip" to "one way." She wouldn't be coming back. Not any time in the near future.

After choosing the date, she scrolled through the options that came up. If she flew economy, she could get out there on less than two hundred dollars. Not bad.

The two thousand she'd had in her checking account had grown to twenty-six hundred, even after paying for food, thanks to her sisters putting her on the Ashbaugh

Charters' payroll and the money she'd gotten scrapping her car. That should tide her over until she got a job if she found a cheap enough place to stay.

Maybe she should check the average cost of rent out there before making her final decision. She opened a new tab and typed her question into the search bar.

Over three thousand dollars? O-kay. That was a little more than she'd expected. At least, if she wound up sleeping in the park the first winter, she wouldn't freeze to death.

She clicked back to the Kayak window as the front door swung open and Kris walked in.

Kris wished her good morning and stopped in front of the desk. "What are you working on?"

"Purchasing an airline ticket."

"To where?"

"I haven't decided yet, but I'm leaning toward San Francisco."

"Why?"

"Because it's warm."

Kris crossed her arms. "So is Pensacola."

"No one in San Francisco is trying to kill me."

"How do you know the people trying to kill you here won't follow you there?"

"I don't, but I have to do something." She dragged the backpack onto her lap and pulled out her wallet.

Kris stepped around the desk. "Hold on. Have you talked to Spence?"

"I don't need to. You know the attack I told you guys about last night? That wasn't the only one."

"You were attacked on the way home, with Jared following?"

"No. A little after midnight, someone kicked in the back door. The only reason I'm alive right now is because Spence was outside with Apollo when it happened and saw the guy break in. He got to him just as he was ready to climb the stairs."

She slid her debit card from her wallet

and plopped it on the desk. If there was a way to pay cash for her airline ticket, she'd do it.

Kris put a hand on her shoulder. "Just slow down. Your charging off into the sunset without a plan isn't a good idea."

"I have a plan. It's called *Get Out of Pensacola.*"

Kris heaved a sigh and stalked out the door. Where was she going? Probably to get Spence. It wasn't going to do her any good.

Alyssa viewed the options presented on the screen. An early to midafternoon flight would work. She could arrive at the airport in plenty of time to get through security and make it to the gate well before boarding.

She chose a flight and clicked on Get Deals. After reading what was there, she hovered over Accept Restrictions. One of those restrictions was no changes, likely typical for low-cost fares. Once she finalized the purchase, she wouldn't be able to change her mind. Well, she could, but she'd be kissing almost two hundred dollars goodbye.

By the time her sister walked past the front window a few minutes later, Alyssa had made it to the screen to enter her payment information. When Kris walked in the door, Spence was right behind her, Apollo next to him. He was still dressed in the shorts and T-shirt he'd been wearing when he'd saved her life last night. Judging from how his hair was sticking up every which way, he hadn't been out of bed long enough to even run a brush through it.

While Kris stood back, Spence charged around the desk to stand next to her.

"What are you doing?"

The question was similar to the one Kris had asked, but his tone said he knew exactly what she was doing and wasn't happy about it.

"Booking a flight out of here." She looked up at him, annoyed that *he* seemed so annoyed. "Last night, even you agreed I needed to leave."

"I said you needed to go somewhere safe."

"That's exactly what I'm doing."

"Not without me, you're not."

She heaved a sigh. Decisions would be a lot easier without all these people trying to "help" her. "You can't go with me. In case you've forgotten, you're in the middle of getting a store set up. You've got merchandise coming next week."

"I can put it on hold."

"You think the company that gave you the business loan will let you put those payments on hold, too?"

He winced. Yep, she'd hit on something he wasn't going to be able to explain away so easily.

He frowned. "Trying to go it alone isn't the solution."

"Do you have another one?" She rose from the chair, giving him all of two seconds to answer. "Didn't think so."

Kris finally stepped closer. "With everything you've told us, these guys really need to be behind bars."

"I totally agree with you. But as far as I'm concerned, as long as they leave me out of it, they can keep doing what they're doing. So, some rich person loses a valuable piece of art and the insurance company has to cover it. Do you really think I care? Not to be selfish or anything, but I don't have a dog in this fight. I'm more interested in staying alive."

Kris's eyes narrowed. Alyssa crossed her arms. Ms. High and Mighty obviously didn't like what she'd just said.

Alyssa nailed her with a stern glare. "Be honest. When I'm gone, you and Kassie will just be relieved to get back to your own lives and not have to deal with your wayward little sister's problems anymore."

Kris matched Alyssa's stance. "You know what your problem is? You think you got dealt a bad hand, and now you're mad at the world. Having our mother disappear when we were teenagers was the pits. But you need to remember she didn't leave us by choice. The day she was murdered, she'd planned for all four of us to run away together. You need to step away from what her disappearance did to your mind and try to get your head on straight. It's time to get rid of the chip on your shoulder."

Alyssa opened her mouth to argue but then snapped it shut again. She didn't have a good comeback because, deep inside, she had to admit Kris was right. She just didn't know what to do about it. That chip had been there so long, she'd probably be lost without it.

Spence cleared his throat, likely trying to keep the argument from getting any further out of hand. "Let's come up with a plan. If you were alone in San Francisco, with absolutely no one watching your back, what would you do if Peter found you?"

Her chest tightened at the thought. "I don't know."

"If you stay here, I'll sleep on the couch downstairs. I'll even send Apollo up to sleep with you."

She shook her head. "I can't take him away from you. You need him."

"But he'll alert us both if someone climbs up onto the balcony. We can also get units to drive by, keep an eye on the place." He smiled. "You're the future sister-in-law of two of Pensacola's finest. If anyone can get protection around here, it should be you."

She sank back into the chair and looked at the computer screen. A few more fields to fill in, and she could be on a plane this afternoon, on her way to a new life in San Francisco.

But Spence was right. What if Peter found out where she'd gone and followed her? There would be no Spence to intervene, no Jared or Tony to have her back.

In trying to go where she thought he

couldn't get to her, she would instead make it easy for him.

Like handing him her life on one of La Maison's silver platters.

NINE

Alyssa stood at the stove in the kitchenette in the back of the charter office, two pots in front of her. One held spaghetti sauce, the other pasta. A good meal for a Sunday evening.

More than a week had passed since the two attempts on her life at Gallery Night. Since then, Spence had camped out nights on the couch in the charter office and had only gone back to his apartment or store if either Jared or Tony was with her.

Units had been patrolling the area en force, driving past on Government Street and circling the parking lot behind the building on a regular basis.

The guy Spence had held at gunpoint until Jared could arrive and arrest him wasn't talking. At least, he wasn't giving them what they wanted to know. His claims that he'd been breaking in, looking for money or stuff to pawn, didn't hold water, especially with the bite marks Alyssa had left on his palm when he'd tried to abduct her earlier.

The fact that there had been no threats for almost nine days didn't coax Alyssa into believing she could let down her guard. In fact, it had done just the opposite. Peter was planning something. After so many failed attempts, he would make sure this time, whatever he did, he would succeed.

The timer on the microwave beeped and she turned the burner off under the pasta, ready to drain it. Right now, she was alone, just briefly. Five minutes ago, Spence had received a call from a delivery driver that the truck was sitting in front of his store, ready to offload some merchandise he had ordered.

Not wanting to be tied up in the middle

of preparing dinner, she had let him out the front, locked the door behind him and set the alarm. He'd even left Apollo with her.

She removed the lid on the sauce and stirred it. It smelled good. It looked good, too, with chunks of meat, mushrooms, onions and green pepper. Cooking for Spence the past week had been fun. He seemed to love everything she had prepared for him. A few times, they had cooked together.

It had also been difficult, a keen reminder of the future she had envisioned so many years ago—the love of her life at her side, nothing ugly ever coming between them, the confidence that they would always be there for each other, no matter what.

She shrugged off the wistful thoughts. Childhood dreams rarely remained intact through the harsh realities of life. And trying to reconstruct those splintered pieces years later was an exercise in futility.

The mental tough talk wasn't doing anything to tamp down what she was feeling for Spence. The truth was, she was dangerously close to falling in love with him all over again, and her heart was ignoring every rational argument she presented.

Spence obviously wasn't having the same problem. If he felt anything for her beyond friendship, he was doing a great job of hiding it. Throughout their time together, he'd shown concern, even fierce protectiveness. He'd been real about his struggles, sharing things that he had likely shared with few, if any, others. But not once had he offered the slightest hint that he had any desire to step over that friendship line.

Alyssa glanced at the clock hanging on the wall. At a little after seven, it wasn't horribly late, but dinner was ready. She hoped Spence made it back before the sauce got cold or overcooked.

She pulled a chair away from the kitchen table and sat. Apollo plodded up to her, and she scratched him behind and under the ears. "Daddy's being a slowpoke, isn't he?"

Apollo wagged his tail, and she laughed. "You agree, don't you? We'll have to see what we can do about it."

The cabin fever was back. Knowing she had no choice had made it even worse. Last night, she had half-heartedly talked to Spence about taking her to church this morning. Twisting her hair up on her head and covering it with a baseball cap hadn't worked, but she'd said she would come up with something else, possibly even find a pair of big, gaudy sunglasses that would hide the upper half of her face.

Spence had said, "No way." She hadn't expected any different. But that had shown how desperate she was about going outside.

As a concession, Spence had brought up the live stream of the service so they could watch it on the computer. That wasn't at all what she'd been looking for. She was still trapped inside, and because she had opened her big mouth, she'd been stuck sitting through a church service.

Once it was over, though, she couldn't complain. It hadn't been near the imposition she had feared. She'd enjoyed the music. It was upbeat, and she recognized two of the songs as ones Spence had played and sung for her on those nights she'd had trouble sleeping.

The pastor's sermon had been good, too. In fact, she hadn't even had to poke herself to avoid falling asleep. Maybe it was because the message had hit her right between the eyes.

He'd preached about Saul's experience on the road to Damascus. She knew the story from those years her mother had taken her to church. The focus of this message, though, was change—Saul's life before his encounter with Jesus versus after. In fact, the change had been so great, God had given him a new name. It was no longer just an ancient story that had happened to someone who'd lived almost two thousand years ago. The pastor had made it relevant to today.

Alyssa had seen some of that change up close. Both her sisters had, in recent years, recommitted their lives to God. Kassie had been first, followed by Kris fairly recently. Alyssa had to admit, there was a distinct difference in the women they were now and the girls they'd been as teenagers.

She had attributed their newfound joy and contentment to both of their statuses as fiancées. But maybe it went deeper than that. Maybe they'd found a sense of contentment that transcended present circumstances, whatever those might be. Their attitude toward her seemed different, too. What she'd thought was judgment over the past couple of weeks, in hindsight, she now saw for what it was—concern.

Even Spence, with all of his struggles, seemed to have an underlying sense of peace that hadn't been there before. It was especially evident when he was playing and singing worship songs.

The pastor had invited everyone to experience that change, to move from "before Christ" to "after Christ." It had sounded really appealing, because whatever she'd been searching for over the past ten years, she hadn't found it.

The lock rattled up front and the sustained tone of the alarm drifted down the hall, followed by four beeps as Spence entered the code. A half minute later, he appeared in the open doorway of the kitchen.

Apollo padded over to greet him, and Alyssa rose from the chair "All good?"

"Yep, everything's accounted for and signed off on. That shipment, anyway. I've got a couple more coming this week."

Over the past few days, there had been a lot of changes next door—shelving installed, brackets for displaying guitars and other merchandise, racks for music books, as well as corkboards for hooks that would hold cables, adapters, picks and any other miscellaneous pieces and parts. The security company had finished installing his alarm system on Friday, so all the new stuff he was buying would be protected. He was shooting for an October 14 open date, a little more than two weeks away. It looked like he was going to make it.

"Perfect timing. Dinner is ready." She turned to the fridge and removed two bowls of salad she had made earlier and covered with plastic wrap.

When everything was on the table, he took both of her hands in his and offered a prayer of thanks, for both the food and God's protection. When the danger was over and they each got back to their own lives, having meals together at night was something she would miss.

She would miss his prayers, too. His saying grace before dinner had gone from something she'd tolerated to something she appreciated.

They had just finished eating when the distant squeal of an alarm sent her heart into her throat. She sprang from her chair.

Spence did, too, but held up a hand. "That's not here. It's not loud enough."

He was right. She inhaled some calming breaths, waiting for her heart rate to return to normal.

"It might be at my place, though. Stay here. I'm going to walk up front and check."

When he returned a minute later, the alarm was still squealing.

"Someone broke the window right beside my front door. I don't know if they got inside."

"Aren't you going to check it out?"

"It's monitored, so the police will be here any minute. Everything in there is covered by insurance. Even if it wasn't, there's nothing in there important enough for me to leave you unprotected."

"But you—" She snapped her mouth shut. He'd left her inside with the alarm and his dog while accepting his delivery. But this was different. Instead of an expected delivery, this was a broken window. It could be random, or it could be someone's way to draw him away and leave her unprotected.

"Stay back here. I don't want anyone to be able to take potshots at you through the front window." Of course, she'd been doing that for the past week, handling her clerical duties in the back office, only slipping through the lobby to head upstairs after he had checked to make sure no one appeared to be milling around outside, watching the building.

He stepped into the hallway, where he could keep an eye on her while still having a view of the edge of the front window. Two or three minutes later, the police arrived.

"They're here. I see the blue lights. I know the police will be right out front, but I'm still setting the alarm and locking the door on my way out."

"Thanks." She would clean up their dinner mess and try not to speculate on who had broken the window or why.

When Apollo started to follow him, he held up a hand. "Stay."

The dog turned and moved to stand at her side. As Spence walked to the front, she scooped the leftover sauce into a plastic container and placed the pan in the sink to fill with water.

The next moment, the crack of splitting wood sent a bolt of panic through her. Apollo charged from the room in a frenzy of barking. When Alyssa ran into the hallway, two men were already inside. One held a pole and was trying to work the loop on the end of it around Apollo's neck. The dog protested with growls interspersed with ferocious barks.

The other man had slipped past them and was headed right for her. The alarm next door was still squealing.

She ran toward the front. She would never be able to get the door unlocked and open before they caught her, but maybe she could catch the attention of Spence or the police.

The man tackled her before she could even reach the end of the hallway. She went down with a crash, and he landed on top of her. Pain shot through her left arm, which was trapped under her. She released a scream, but a large hand cut it short.

The weight on her lessened and disappeared altogether. Then an arm slid around her waist and lifted her from the floor. Just before being spun around, she caught a glimpse of the front window. A police officer was framed in its left-hand edge. He was standing in profile to her, oblivious to her predicament.

The alarm outside fell silent, but it was too late. The hand over her mouth was firmly in place, thumb and index finger pinching her nose so she couldn't even breathe. Biting him was impossible, too. He'd cupped his palm. Maybe he'd learned from the other guy. Or maybe he was smarter.

As he carried her down the hall, she kicked and fought as hard as she could, desperate for air. Her struggles did as much good as they had in the alley. Peter's thugs were far too strong for her.

At the end of the hall, angry barks came from behind the closed bathroom door. The second man waited at the door, his hands now empty of the pole he had held earlier.

When her abductor stepped outside, a white cargo van was waiting in the parking lot, back doors open. Rather than being pulled into a space, its rear end faced the building. The engine was running, the driver in the front ready to take off.

The man tossed her inside and hopped in after her. She sucked in several frantic gasps of air and then released another scream as the doors slammed shut. Moments later, the front passenger door opened, and the man who had restrained Apollo climbed into the seat. The van took off before he even got the door shut.

Alyssa pushed herself into a seated position, fighting against the lurching of the vehicle. It squealed from the parking lot and then turned away from Palafox. The glow of streetlights shone through the windshield and the two front side windows. The cargo portion of the van was windowless.

Her gaze landed on the driver's face, framed in the rearview mirror—dark eyes, tanned skin, masculine features bordered by black hair.

Her heart almost stopped.

She was looking at Peter.

"Alyssa!" Spence ran through the charter office, Braydon right behind him. They'd just heard a scream. It had sounded as if it had come from somewhere behind the building.

He hadn't taken the time to unlock the door. Instead, he'd kicked it in. He would deal with that later.

The hopes that the scream he'd heard had nothing to do with Alyssa died with his first glance down the hallway. The back door was wide open, leaning against the hallway wall at an unnatural angle.

Muffled barks came from the back, along with another sound—running water. Ignoring his dog, who was currently closed up in the bathroom, and the water running in the kitchen, he shot out the back door and into the parking lot.

A total of four cars occupied the spaces. All of the vehicles were vacant. No one was standing around in the lot or even walking past. He spun to run back inside and almost plowed into Braydon.

"They've got Alyssa. We need to call it in, put out a BOLO."

While Braydon radioed the dispatcher, Spence paced. The officer's description was spot-on. Thick red hair, waist-length, about five-four, medium build. When he gave her name as Alyssa Ashbaugh, Spence didn't correct him.

Braydon lowered the radio. "Any idea what kind of vehicle we're looking for?"

"No." He couldn't even say for sure

they'd taken her away in a vehicle. "Can we get people checking the area, seeing if they notice anything unusual?"

It was a long shot. Knowing police were standing right out front, the likelihood of the men dragging her away on foot was nonexistent.

Braydon finished the latest request, and Spence looked around. "What about security cameras on the surrounding businesses?" Cameras on Palafox wouldn't be any help. The suspects would have avoided that route. But maybe on Church Street behind, or one of the side streets.

Braydon nodded. "We'll get business owners to check the footage and see if there were any suspicious vehicles, or anyone that appeared to be leaving in a hurry about five minutes ago. It might give us a starting point."

When Spence turned back toward the building, the barks coming from inside finally registered again, reminding him his dog was trapped in the bathroom.

Poor Apollo was probably beside himself, knowing Alyssa needed help and he couldn't get to her.

Actually, Spence needed help himself. A lead weight filled his gut, and his chest was so tight, he was finding it hard to breathe. He'd thought Alyssa would be safer tucked away in the back of the office than standing out front in full view of anyone driving past.

He'd been wrong. The broken window at his store had been nothing but a decoy, a way to distract him so he would leave Alyssa unguarded just long enough for them to move in. Now Peter's goons had her, if not Peter himself.

He had almost reached the damaged door of the charter office when Jared charged out with Justice.

"I heard the call. I've let Kassie know. She's going to call Kris and Tony. The authorities are doing everything they can to find her, and Kris and Kassie will be on their knees. Tony will be praying, too, but

I'm guessing he'll be putting himself back on duty."

"Good. I've got to let Apollo out."

Jared followed him inside. "I'm guessing it was Alyssa's kidnappers who locked him in there. I'm surprised he allowed it."

Actually, Spence was, too. Apollo wasn't a trained guard dog, but the Lab had always been protective of him. Lately, he'd displayed the same protectiveness toward Alyssa.

When he opened the bathroom door, Apollo sprang toward him, dragging an aluminum pole with a metal noose at one end. That noose was around his neck.

"Poor boy." Spence cupped his dog's face in his hands and then tried to break the noose.

Jared stepped up beside him. "Here. Let me help."

He slid his hand up the pole. Upon finding a slide release, he gave it a sharp pull. One side of the noose fell away and Apollo was instantly free.

Jared then stepped into the kitchen and shut off the faucet. Alyssa apparently hadn't stopped up the sink. There was no water overflowing onto the floor.

Braydon walked inside, giving Jared a brief nod before addressing Spence. "One of the officers is trying to reach business owners in the area to view security camera footage. We've got units patrolling, looking for anything suspicious. Surrounding counties are being alerted, also."

Spence swallowed past a large lump in his throat. Police were patrolling but had no idea what they were looking for. Having Alyssa's description didn't do them much good in the dark. Unless the driver did something careless, there would be no reason to stop him.

The hopelessness of her situation bore down on him. He needed to do something.

"I'm leaving to go look for her."

Jared lifted his eyebrows. "Where are you going?"

"I don't know, but if I just stand around

and wait for word, I'll go crazy. I'm going to get on I-65 and drive toward Montgomery. Maybe the men who abducted her are headed back to Atlanta to turn her over to Peter."

"That sounds like a good plan."

No, it didn't. It was a long shot. But since no one had any better ideas, that was what Spence would go with. That and lots of unceasing prayer.

After grabbing his weapon and Apollo's leash, he headed for the door. "Apollo, come." On his way out, he cast Jared a glance over one shoulder. "Please keep me posted on any developments. Kassie and Kris both have my number." They'd collected it when he'd signed the lease on the store.

He moved toward the Forester at an uncomfortable jog, favoring his left leg. Apollo trotted in front of him, excitement rippling through him, as if he sensed they were headed out to find Alyssa and bring her back.

As soon as he opened the SUV's back door, Apollo jumped in, not waiting for the command. The dog was as anxious as he was.

He pulled from the parking lot and drove toward Interstate 110. That would take him to I-65. He would keep his eyes peeled for anything suspicious and stay in touch with the police through Jared. Maybe one of those security cameras would actually let him know what he was looking for.

Why had the men taken her? Were they going to kill her in the vehicle and dump her body? Or were they waiting until they got far enough outside town that there wouldn't be any witnesses?

Something didn't add up, though. If all they'd wanted to do was kill her, shooting her inside the charter office would have been a lot faster and less risky than kidnapping her.

Maybe they had other plans for her.

A sense of dread pressed down on him. One man was dead, and two others were behind bars. Peter and his cronies probably weren't happy. If they decided Alyssa needed to pay for making things so difficult for them—no, he wouldn't even allow his thoughts to go there.

God, please protect her. Please let someone find her before it's too late.

TEN

Alyssa sat on the floor of the van, propped against the driver's-side wall. She wasn't comfortable. The floor was hard and what she was leaning against offered no support for her back. But she had no choice. Both rear seats had been removed.

The men hadn't bothered to tie her up. They probably hadn't seen the need. There were three of them and one of her. Peter was occupied with driving, but it wasn't any consolation. Before they'd even reached the interstate, he had taken a weapon from his side and laid it in a cubby in the dash. It was close enough for her to see, but not close enough for her to grab, even if she knew what to do with it. She didn't.

As far as the other two, either of them could have smashed her like a bug. They were both as big as the guys who had accosted her at Gallery Night.

Currently, they were on Interstate 10, headed west. They had passed into Alabama some time ago and had to be nearing the Mississippi border by now. Since leaving Pensacola, they had entered plenty of wooded areas where they could have stopped, marched her through the trees and shot her.

Instead, Peter had kept driving. What plans did he have for her?

Not knowing was about to make her crazy. For the past hour, her brain had been concocting all kinds of scenarios, ways Peter could make her pay for the inconvenience she'd been to him. How many men had he sent after her before he'd finally decided to deal with the situation himself?

He was probably furious. Except, he was hiding it well. Actually, she had no idea how Peter displayed anger. She'd never witnessed it. Something told her he was too controlled to fly into a rage about anything. His anger would be much more dangerous—cold, hard and lethal.

Another wave of fear swept through her. She couldn't stand it anymore. She leaned forward to look at him in the rearview mirror.

"Where are you taking me?"

His gaze met hers. That brief eye contact told her he knew the question was for him.

His attention shifted back to the road. Seconds stretched into a half minute or more, the silence broken only by the rumble of the van's engine and the noise of the road beneath her.

Frustration took the edge off some of the fear. "All the effort you and your men have expended in the past couple of weeks is ridiculous. I walked in and heard you guys discussing paintings. Do you think I care? I don't even care if you and your buddies are fencing stolen art."

More of that exasperating silence. Why didn't he say something?

"Look, you probably know me well enough to realize I'm not one to play the hero. You know the strong sense of justice that makes certain people think they have to right everything wrong in the world? I don't have it. Never have. My causes are things that impact me directly. Like trying to avoid trouble, keeping out of other people's business...staying alive."

Still no response. If she climbed over the console and tried to shake him, he'd probably shoot her.

Maybe she could appeal to whatever feelings he might have had for her. "What about all the things you told me? How I'm different...how you've never met anyone like me?"

"Everything I said was true. You *are* different. You didn't seem that impressed with me. As my waitress, you were friendly but had just enough attitude to make things interesting. You turned me down for a solid three weeks before you would even agree to let me buy you dinner. I've never had a woman do that."

Yeah, he probably hadn't. It wasn't just his looks or even how he exuded success. He had a magnetism about him that drew attention wherever he went. She'd seen the looks he'd received when they'd been out. Instead of jealousy, she'd felt pride and amazement that she'd been the one to land such a prize. Right now, she'd gladly trade places with any one of those women.

"If you think I'm special, then why don't you let me go?"

"My associates would never go for that."

"They don't have to know. I was looking at airline tickets this morning, ready to choose a big city where I could get lost in the crowd. I'd keep my mouth shut and you'd never hear from me again."

"No go. You'd always be a loose end." He shook his head. "You should have stayed in the car like I told you."

"I know that now, but it's not like I can go back and change the past."

"No, you can't."

Despair settled over her. There was no talking Peter out of whatever he was going to do. She was right back where she'd been before she'd begun this conversation—scared half out of her mind, wondering where he was taking her and what he planned to do with her when they got there.

Alyssa heaved a sigh. "Then why don't you just kill me and dump my body?"

"That was my plan after you walked in on our meeting. I'd already put the tracking device on your car and sent requests to all of your friends on social media, just in case something like this happened. Even though you weren't very active and hadn't gotten around to changing your status to 'in a relationship,' the fact you were a mutual friend was enough to get quite a few of them to accept my request. Brandi Feldman was one of those."

She waited for him to continue. He'd said that *was* his plan. Apparently, it wasn't any longer. What was it now?

When he didn't continue, she prodded him. "You said killing me *was* your plan. It isn't any longer?"

"With one man dead and two others arrested, my buddies and I decided death is too good for you."

Too good? What could be worse than death?

God, please help me. Right on the tail of the silent plea came the thought that God wasn't even listening. After all, why would He? She hadn't paid Him much mind *before* her mother had disappeared. Afterward, she'd turned her back on everything her mother had tried to pass on, including her faith.

But when Spence had cried for God to save him, God had come through. Spence had said he wasn't sure if it was all right to bargain with God. It had turned out all right for him. Better than all right.

God, if You help me get out of this, I'll...
What? Spence had promised to commit
the rest of his life to God. He'd picked up
his guitar and used his talents by serving
on his church's worship team.

Was she ready to go that far? Music
was out of the question. Kassie was the
only musically gifted one in the family.
What about nursery duty? Teaching Sunday school? Cleaning toilets? Spence had
said if someone did decide to bargain with
God, they'd better be prepared to come
through on whatever they promised.

Before she could ponder it further, the
van gradually decreased speed. Her pulse
did the opposite. Was Peter getting ready
to pull over? Maybe exit the interstate?
Why?

She sat straight and craned her neck.
The turn signal came on, and her heart
pounded harder. The van continued to de-
celerate. An exit sign sped past the passenger window. After a stop and a couple

of turns, Peter pulled under a gas station canopy.

It wasn't a Pilot or Love's, or one of the other large stations. In fact, based on what shone through the front windshield, it wasn't even that well lit.

The passenger door swung open, and Peter handed the man a wad of bills. A few minutes after he disappeared, she heard the sound of the pump nozzle being inserted into the fuel filler behind her. Within a few minutes, he would be finished and they would once again hit the road. This might be her only chance to summon help.

She looked at Peter in the mirror. "I need to go to the bathroom."

"You'll have to wait."

"I won't make it much longer. I drank a bunch of tea with dinner." When he didn't respond, she continued. "I don't know who this van belongs to, but they might have a problem with you returning it with stains or unpleasant odors."

Peter turned around to look at the man who had ridden on the floor opposite her. "Go scope it out."

The man gave him a salute and climbed from the back. When he returned a minute later holding a long, thin piece of wood with a small chain and key dangling from one end, her heart fell. There would be no chance of whispering a plea for help to another occupant.

The man raised the hand holding the stick. "The restroom is around the side. It needs a key to get in."

"Go ahead and take her. Make sure she doesn't try anything."

She climbed from the van and, before he allowed her to step from between the two open doors, the man patted her down. Then he pulled a switchblade from his front jeans' pocket. At the press of a button, the blade burst from the end.

After a quick glance at the license plate, she walked toward the building, silently reciting the combination of six letters and numbers over and over. She looked around her. She'd been right. The station was small, even smaller than she had guessed. The canopy wasn't much bigger than a residential carport, with one double-sided pump where a maximum of two vehicles could fill up at any time. Currently, the van was the only vehicle there.

The cashier manning the tiny convenience store watched them through the front window as they approached. He was a young guy, probably around her age. Under the bright fluorescents, his features held alertness.

Alyssa's thoughts raced as she tried to figure out a way to signal that she was in trouble. She had just started to mouth the word *help* when he turned away.

At light pressure against her lower back, she stiffened. The man behind her leaned close. "If you even think about trying anything, you'll feel this blade in your right kidney."

She picked up her pace, dismissing her

previous thoughts of escape. She wasn't giving up, though. She would just have to think of something else.

After continuing past the first door marked Men, the man unlocked the second one and held it open while she stepped inside. She wrinkled her nose against the odor of urine, thankful she had no intention of using that toilet.

Once the door had swung closed, she turned the lock. Since the man guarding her still had the key, the action wouldn't accomplish anything except possibly buy her a second or two while he fiddled with the lock.

She looked frantically around the space, patting her pockets. They were empty. Of course they were. The man had already patted her down and found nothing. She had no lipstick or pens. Not even a coin to scratch a message in the paint covering the concrete-block walls. A toilet occupied one corner, a small, overflowing trash can next to it. On the opposite wall, a sink and countertop sat atop a two-foot cabinet. There was absolutely nothing she could use to fashion a cry for help.

Or maybe there was. She pulled a long length of toilet paper from the roll and tore off individual squares. The next step was to roll each of them into strips for use in forming letters.

She couldn't lay out her message in the middle of the floor. The man waiting just outside would likely see it as soon as she tried to exit. But there was about a two-foot space in the back corner, hidden from the view of the door by the sink cabinet.

Clutching her rolled-up sheets of toilet paper in one hand, she squatted and started laying them out. The first four formed a *W*. Next to that, she placed two vertical sheets and laid a third horizontally between them, forming an *H*. Next was a *T*.

At a loud knock on the door, she had to stifle a shriek.

"Hurry it up in there. We don't have all night."

"I'm almost done." She flushed the toilet.

Hopefully, the next person who walked in would recognize her abbreviation for *white*.

"Washing my hands. I'll be right out."

After turning on the water, she squatted again and spelled out *VAN* below the other three letters. Next would be the tag number.

She rose again and turned off the water. "Drying my hands now." She pulled two paper towels from the dispenser before squatting again.

She had gotten only the first three characters of the tag number spelled out when the knock came again, louder and angrier than before.

The lock rattled. "Time's up. I'm coming in."

She threw the last pieces of toilet paper against the wall and sprang to her feet. As the door swung open, she wadded up the paper towels she had torn off earlier. He took a step toward her, one arm extended, ready to grab her.

"I'm coming." She had to keep him from stepping any farther into the bathroom. If he saw what she'd been trying to do… whatever would happen, it wouldn't be good.

She hurried to the open doorway, throwing the wadded paper towels in the trash on her way past, hoping he wouldn't notice they weren't wet.

As she stepped outside, he grabbed her by the arm. "Lock the door."

She twisted the lock.

"Now, you're going to hold my hand while we walk back to the van. That guy inside was watching us a little too closely for my liking. We're going to get rid of any suspicions."

He grasped her hand, intertwining his fingers with hers, and she suppressed a shudder. Instead of taking her to the back of the vehicle again, he walked her around between the van and the pump, and opened the side door. After he had shut her inside, he disappeared again and returned a minute later without the bathroom key.

As Peter cranked the van, she closed her eyes. *God, please let someone see my message and call the police.* It likely wouldn't happen until tomorrow. The dinky, out-of-the-way place surely wouldn't be open twenty-four hours. The likelihood of someone else stopping to get gas tonight was slim. It was even less likely someone would ask for the key to the ladies' room.

Maybe one of tasks on the clerk's list of closing responsibilities was to check the bathroom. The time had to be after ten. The station would likely be closing within the next hour.

Peter put the van into gear and pulled away from the pump. Instead of going out the way he had come in, he circled around behind the station. She could guess what he was doing. He was making sure the clerk couldn't read the tag number from inside the store.

The way back to the interstate involved more turns than the trip to the station. Soon, Peter was accelerating up the on-ramp. "No more stops till we get there." The statement was stern and seemed to be aimed at all of them.

So they were headed somewhere specific. Where exactly was "there"? By now, they had to be getting close to Mississippi.

Finally, Peter pressed a cell phone to his ear. "I'm headed your way with an Irène Cahen."

Alyssa looked around the van, all the while knowing she wouldn't find any paintings in there. The entire cargo area was empty except for herself and the man who had taken her to the restroom.

She was familiar with the painting Peter had mentioned. *Irène Cahen d'Anvers*, a Renoir. Peter had it. She'd seen it in his place. Actually, it was a quality reproduction. The original would be well out of even Peter's price range.

Peter laughed before continuing. "A lot of spunk."

Huh? He could tell that from a painting? The girl looked sweet and demure with her hands folded in her lap, her long, red hair flowing over her shoulder.

Long. Red. Hair.

The three words punched into her. *Dear God, no.* She shook her head, trying to rattle loose the realization that had lodged itself in her mind.

Long, red hair. Young, though not nearly as young as the real Irène Cahen D'Anvers. Peter and his buddies weren't fencing stolen art. They were involved in human trafficking. All art aficionados, they made a game out of naming their victims based on famous portraits of women.

She was the Irène Cahen Peter mentioned.

She put her face in her hands, hopelessness washing through her. She had a longtime history of choosing losers. She had thought she'd finally done well for herself. Instead, she'd made the biggest mistake of her life.

Suddenly, Peter jerked the wheel to the right and braked so hard she had to thrust out one arm to keep from rolling across the floor of the van.

The man on the floor with her did the same. "Whoa, dude. I thought you said no more stops till we get there."

"The overpass about a half mile back, there were a bunch of police cars, lights flashing. They may have been headed to the interstate. Unless Alyssa pulled something at our last stop, it's not likely they have anything to do with us, but I'm not taking any chances."

The man across from her grinned. "That's why we work for you."

Alyssa closed her eyes again as cautious hope trickled through her. Peter was right. Those police cars may have had nothing to do with them. But there was also a chance someone had seen her message, and every agency in Alabama or Mississippi or wherever they were, was searching for a white van with a tag number that began K6J.

Over the next few minutes, Peter made several turns. Finally, he stopped and killed the engine. Judging from the scarce light finding its way through the windows, they were in a neighborhood, or possibly a business district where everything had shut down some time ago.

Peter once again put the phone to his ear. "We've had a little delay, but we'll be there with the merchandise before morning."

His words put a knot of dread in the pit of her stomach, knowing she was the merchandise. Whether the police cars had anything to do with her or not, the delay had to be a good thing. Maybe someone would question the van sitting alone in the dark and call the police to check it out.

God, please send someone.

She leaned her head back against the side of the van, and the minutes ticked by—fifteen minutes, a half hour, longer. Maybe. With no way to judge it, her time estimates were just that—estimates.

Her eyelids began to feel heavy. There was no way she would sleep. But she could rest. The events of the evening had drained her, and she still didn't know what lay ahead.

Her thoughts grew erratic, and she had the sensation of floating…drifting…

Reality slammed into her, and a startled gasp escaped. The man sitting across from her snickered.

Peter made another phone call. "We're getting back on the road now. We'll be at the port within the hour. Don't ship out the rest of the merchandise until I arrive."

He ended the call and dropped the phone into the console. Two words from his short conversation echoed in her mind: *port* and *ship*.

Alyssa had thought it couldn't get any worse. It just had.

By morning, she was going to be on her

way to another country with other trafficking victims to be sold into slavery.

Peter was right. The fate she was facing
would be worse than death.

ELEVEN

Spence sped along I-10, praying harder than he had ever prayed. Apollo lay in the seat behind him and whimpered. The whimpering had been happening off and on for the past two hours.

So had his occasional attempts to climb over the console and get into his lap. Just what he needed—a seventy-five-pound dog in his lap while driving down the interstate at seventy miles an hour.

The problem was, Apollo was picking up on Spence's anxiety, and it was killing him to not be able to do what he was trained to do. Spence didn't even want him riding in the front passenger seat. In case of an accident, the dog could sail right through the windshield. So, until they stopped, Apollo would have to remain in the back seat, as difficult as it might be for both of them.

The security cameras within a two-block radius of the charter office hadn't captured anything of value. Peter's men had probably already scoped out the area before abducting Alyssa and had figured out how to avoid them.

An hour ago, though, authorities had gotten a break. A clerk at a small gas station had reported a message spelled out in toilet paper on the floor of the women's restroom. It had included a vague vehicle description and the first three digits of a tag number.

The clerk had been able to add another detail to "white van." It was a cargo van, the kind that was windowless except for the windshield and two front side windows. He'd seen it pull up, had watched as a man and woman made their way to the ladies' room on the exterior of the building, the man holding the key he'd given him.

He'd been able to give a description of the two people. The man was large, a good ten inches taller than the woman, and far heavier. The long, red hair he'd described on the woman had left Spence no doubt. He'd been looking at Alyssa.

Spelling out a cry for help using toilet paper would be just the kind of thing Alyssa would think of in dire circumstances. She'd always been intelligent in a street-smart kind of way. Intelligent, beautiful, compassionate and witty. Confident, but with an underlying vulnerability that few people ever saw. That vulnerability only endeared her to him even more.

They weren't right for each other, but he loved her with all of his heart. He could no longer deny it.

God, please somehow give me a chance to tell her so.

As soon as he had gotten Jared's call, he'd turned around. Since Alyssa's kidnappers had had a two-hour head start, Spence had no chance of catching them.

But being reasonably sure he was heading in the right direction helped his state of mind. He was at least accomplishing something.

Over the next hour, he continued to drive, interspersing a steady stream of prayers with the Christian music he had pouring into the vehicle through the stereo system. Several times, he had to tamp down an overwhelming urge to call Jared for an update. He didn't need to bug his new friend. If there were any developments, he would have already known. Jared would have called immediately.

He heaved a sigh. He'd passed the Alabama/Mississippi border some time ago. How far ahead of him was the white cargo van? Was it even still on Interstate 10? It could have turned off a long time ago and be headed somewhere north of them.

He glanced at the Forester's gas gauge. He was nearing a quarter of a tank. He'd soon have to stop for gas. That would put him ten or fifteen minutes further behind.

But running out of gas on the interstate could have him stranded for hours.

For the next several minutes, he searched the exits for signs of well-known truck stops, somewhere he could be in and out in the shortest amount of time. In the distance, brake lights lit up the darkness. He eased off the gas, his pulse picking up speed.

The holdup could be unrelated—an accident or road construction. But chances were good the police had set up a road block. Jared had told him a manhunt involving several agencies was underway.

As Spence approached, the clear night offered great visibility on the straight, flat road. Those brake lights extended as far as he could see. He eased to a stop. He wasn't going anywhere for a while.

He checked the gas gauge again. The needle was now touching the one-quarter line. Traffic crept forward about ten feet and stopped again. Was the white van stuck somewhere in this mess? If so, were the men panicking? Their desperation would put Alyssa in even more danger.

Traffic moved again and he eased onto the shoulder. "Come on, Apollo. Let's go find Alyssa."

He stepped from the vehicle and circled to the passenger side to clip the leash to Apollo's collar. If the van was still on I-10, it would be far ahead of them. After sliding his weapon into his waistband and pulling his shirt over it, he sent another plea heavenward and began moving west at a slow jog, a few feet from the shoulder.

Apollo trotted beside him on his right. On his left, traffic continued to creep forward in its steady start-stop rhythm. His pace, even with his bad hip, was considerably faster than the vehicles next to him.

A good quarter mile ahead of him, a vehicle pulled onto the shoulder. Maybe someone else was low on gas. Instead of stopping just off the road, like he'd done, the driver kept going, off the asphalt and into the grass.

Was the vehicle a cargo van? It was too far away to tell. And now it was growing farther away, moving past the stopped vehicles.

Spence kicked his body into an even faster pace, ignoring the pain in his hip. After about a minute, the vehicle's brake lights came on. Instead of waiting to try to cut back into traffic, it moved even farther from the road, right up against the woods.

As he drew closer, the vehicle crept forward again, wheels turned to the left, and stopped. It was definitely a white cargo van, just like the clerk had described. Moments after the vehicle stopped, it reversed direction, backing up against the woods.

Without slowing his pace, Spence pulled his phone from his pocket and dialed 911. His breath came in pants as he explained the situation to the dispatcher.

"Can you give me your location? A mile marker or nearest exit?"

Oh, man. He should have paid more attention before hitting the traffic jam. "There was an exit about a mile back, a numbered road."

"603?"

"I think that might be it."

"I've got you."

Yeah, she was probably tracking him through his mobile location. "The back door on the van just opened."

"Can you see anyone getting out?"

"No. The door's blocking my view."

"How far away are you?"

"About a football field." Too distant to see beneath the door if someone stepped from the back, especially in the dark. The sky was moonless, and none of the headlights shone that far to the side.

But he didn't need great light to figure out what was going on. Alyssa was in that van. Whatever was happening up ahead, the men weren't going to be caught holding her.

"I'm moving closer."

"Stay back. The police are on their way."

He cast a glance over his shoulder. Flashing blue lights were barely visible on the horizon. "I think I see them, but they're too far away." If the men were preparing to march Alyssa into the woods and kill her, those units would never arrive in time.

He ducked closer to the woods and continued his forward movement, ignoring the dispatcher's commands. The nearby engine noise helped to conceal his footsteps, especially the rumble of the semitrucks.

Her voice once again came through the phone. "Where are the police now?" She'd promised to remain on the line with him until the authorities arrived.

"They're closer." Had the men holding Alyssa seen them yet? When they did, they would likely accelerate whatever plans they had for her.

He dropped his voice to a whisper. "I'm leaving the line open so you can still track my movement, but I'm turning down the volume and dropping the phone into my shirt pocket."

"Sir, you need to let the police handle this."

"They won't get here in time." He'd hissed the words. He would love to step back and let the police handle it, because chances were too good that, for Alyssa to live, he was going to have to kill someone.

Once he silenced his phone and dropped it into his pocket, he pulled his pistol from his waistband. Voices drifted to him.

"Take care of her, and make it fast."

"You got it."

Spence crept closer. The van wasn't more than forty feet in front of him now. A figure was moving away from it, deeper into the woods. No, actually it was two figures—a larger one trying to restrain a smaller one. Sticks crunched under heavy footsteps.

Something else reached Spence, too— muffled sounds of protest, feminine in pitch. The men had gagged her so she couldn't scream.

Suddenly, the man who held her stopped and slid a hand into his pocket. As he withdrew something unidentifiable in the darkness, Alyssa took advantage of the moment and twisted away from him. Her hands were tied behind her back.

She hadn't taken more than two steps before he grabbed her again. He lifted his other arm. A gleam of starlight glistened off something metal. It was the blade of a knife.

Spence raised the pistol.

God, make my aim true.

He pulled the trigger. The shot reverberated through the trees. The man jerked. As his knees buckled, he swung the knife in a wide arc. Alyssa went down and rolled away, coming to a stop against a tree a couple of yards from where the man had fallen. Had he cut her?

With his weapon still trained on the unmoving figure on the ground, Spence gave Apollo a pat on the rump. "Go see Alyssa."

His dog charged over to her while Spence carefully approached the man he had shot. He wasn't moving. The entrance wound was barely visible in the poor light. Spence had shot him in the temple. The man was lying on what was probably a nasty exit wound.

Alyssa's laughter erupted behind him— high-pitched, with a hysterical edge that even the gag couldn't hide. Apollo was showering her face with doggy kisses.

After hurrying toward her, Spence removed the gag and untied her hands. She was still laughing.

He extended a hand. "We need to get out of here."

His gunshot was an announcement to anyone in the area that something had happened. There was still at least one man in the van, maybe more. They would come to investigate, if for nothing more than to make sure their witness was dead.

Alyssa's laughter died as quickly as it had started, and her shoulders shook with silent sobs. In fact, her whole body was shaking. She was probably in shock.

Rustling sounded nearby, growing closer. Spence stiffened, aiming his weapon in that direction. He held up an index finger behind him, signaling Alyssa to stay quiet.

There was more rustling, coming from a different direction. Someone was taking a route similar to the one Spence had taken. Actually, it was several someones. Flashlight beams swept through the trees around them.

The first footsteps he'd heard veered away, the gait fast and heavy. A German shepherd police dog flew past, in hot pursuit. A man's agonized scream followed seconds later.

Suddenly, the woods were swarming with law enforcement personnel. Spence called to one near him. "Check the van. There may be more."

"Others already are."

Spence looked at Alyssa, who was still sitting on the ground, her arms wrapped around Apollo, face pressed against his side. "How many are there?"

At her silence, he hurried over to her and dropped to his knees. "Alyssa?"

She was sobbing louder now and shaking even more violently. He drew her into his arms, and she slowly released his dog. "It's okay. You're safe now."

God, please don't let her be hurt.

He still didn't know if she was injured or bleeding.

Finally, she slid her arms around his neck and took a shuddering breath. "He was going to sell me."

Her words sent a jolt all the way to his toes. "What?"

"He was going to sell me. Peter doesn't fence stolen art. He's a human trafficker. He was taking me to a port to be shipped out." Another shudder shook her shoulders.

Suddenly, she leaned back and looked at him, eyes wide. "There are others."

"What do you mean?"

"Peter talked to someone on the phone a few times. One time he told them to not ship out any of the merchandise until he arrived with me."

Spence motioned one of the police officers to come over and relayed what Alyssa had said.

The officer knelt next to them. "Did he say where this port was?"

Alyssa's arms slid from Spence's neck. "No."

"Did he mention any names or anything that might help us find these people?"

"No, that's all."

The officer rose and radioed in the information.

Spence took both of Alyssa's hands in his. "Did they hurt you?"

She shook her head. "They probably didn't want to damage the merchandise. At least, until they decided they had to kill me."

"When you went down, I was afraid he had cut you."

"No, I tried to step back, caught my heel on a tree root and fell. I knew I needed to get out of the reach of the knife."

"You did good." He wrapped her in his arms again. He didn't know if she still needed his comfort. But he needed hers. He'd come so close to losing her tonight.

She didn't protest. Instead, her arms once again encircled his neck. Judging from the way she was holding on, that was exactly where she wanted to be.

He buried his face in her hair. *I love you.* The silent words never made it past his lips. She was in his arms now. But he couldn't speak for tomorrow or the next day, or the day after that. Now that she was free to go anywhere she wanted to go, no danger, no ties, would she want to settle down? Would she even consider returning to her roots, circling right back to where she'd started? Was that even the right thing to do?

He couldn't answer that. She probably couldn't, either.

But, tonight, he didn't have to think about it.

Because, tonight, he wasn't going to let her go.

TWELVE

Three lit candles rose from a base of greenery in the center of the table, and silverware tinged against porcelain plates.

Kris always set a pretty table, especially when dinner included guests. Although all of today's guests, with the exception of Spence, were family. Kris sat next to Tony, little Gavin on her other side, and Kassie and Jared occupied the other side of the table. Alyssa and Spence completed the circle. Apollo lay in one corner, Bella in the other. The seven of them had just finished attending church together. Actually eight, including Apollo.

Two weeks had passed since Peter and his thugs had abducted her. That night, police had swarmed the Port of New

Orleans. As Louisiana's only container port, it had been the most logical starting point. Those efforts had paid off. The authorities had rescued almost four dozen women and children from a container awaiting shipment. Alyssa would likely never meet those trafficking victims, but for the past two weeks, she'd seen them in her dreams—nameless faces, filled with terror then relief as heroes rushed in to snatch them from their fate.

According to Tony and Jared, the authorities had made more than a dozen arrests since then and the investigation was still ongoing. The operation had been much bigger than Peter and the three men she'd seen him with in the back room.

She was still in awe over how God had heard her cries for help. As the man had dragged her into the woods, she'd been sure she was going to die. First, she'd made sure she was ready to face eternity. Then, like Spence, she'd tried to bargain, promising God that if He saved her, she'd commit her life to Him. At the time, she'd had no idea what that would look like. She still didn't. But she was open to the possibilities.

When she'd heard the gunshot and the man holding her had crumpled to his knees, the last thing she had expected was to see Apollo and Spence step into view. Spence hadn't been just *her* answer to prayer that night. He'd probably been the answer to a lot of other prayers—those of the people in the shipping container, as well as their frantic family members.

The fact her abduction had led to all of them being rescued had made everything she'd gone through during those three weeks worth it. Maybe God would redeem her past mistakes by allowing her to help other girls make better choices than she'd made.

Kassie stabbed a bite of meat and held it up. "This is good. Everything is delicious."

Fifteen minutes ago, the large platter in

the center of the table had held roast beef, potatoes and carrots. While they'd been growing up, that had been their traditional Sunday dinner. Early in the morning, their mom would pull out the large roasting pan. She'd brown the meat, sprinkle it with dry onion soup and seasonings, and arrange the potatoes and carrots around it. Then she would put it in the oven and, by the time they'd get home from church, the potatoes and carrots would be tender and the meat would pick apart easily with a fork.

Today's gathering wasn't just to share an after-church meal. It was also Alyssa's farewell dinner.

Kassie continued, the bite still on her fork. "The company is good, too. We need to go back to making this a Sunday tradition. Not that I'm saying you should feed us every week. We could trade off."

Kris nodded. "I agree."

Alyssa would, too, if she were going to stay. Sunday dinnertime around this table was one of the few good memories she carried from her childhood. Attendance had been mandatory, at least for the three girls—no extracurricular activities and no running off with friends. It was family time, and they were going to engage each other like loving family, which meant no arguing or unkind words. They'd usually managed to comply. The fact they'd spent the morning in church probably helped.

Sometimes their dad joined them—for dinner, anyway. Alyssa couldn't remember a single time when he'd gone to church with them. Maybe the idea of sitting in church on Sunday morning and doing drug running during the week hadn't sat well with him.

Kassie grinned. "My cooking isn't as good as yours, but it's hard to mess up roast, potatoes and carrots." She grew serious and her gaze locked with Alyssa's. "You don't have to go."

Both of her sisters had said the same thing, several times. They weren't just doing lip service, either. They really didn't want her to leave. Coming back home had been one of the smartest decisions she'd ever made. Staying wouldn't be.

"Yes, I do."

"Why?"

"I need to make a fresh start, somewhere nobody has any negative expectations."

"You need your family."

She frowned at Kassie. "I don't need a crutch."

Kris heaved an exasperated sigh. "We're not a crutch. We're a support system. That's something everybody needs."

"I've got to prove to myself I can make it on my own."

Kris pressed her lips together. "That's what you've been doing for the past seven years. We saw how well that turned out."

Alyssa sprang to her feet, slapping her palms down on the table. She'd heard enough. "This is exactly what I'm talking about."

Little Gavin pressed one fist to his mouth and started to cry.

Alyssa's heart twisted. "And now I've upset your little boy. Thank you for your hospitality, but I'm calling a cab."

Kris stood and rushed around the table to stop her before she could escape the dining room. "I'm sorry. I didn't mean it like that. Sometimes my filter doesn't work very well."

Alyssa shrugged. "Don't worry about it. This just proves my point. If my own family can't forget my past mistakes, how will anyone else ever see me as anything but a perpetual mess-up?"

"Alyssa, please. That's not what I meant. I was just stressing the importance of having your family around you. Life's a lot easier when you're not trying to go it alone. After being at odds all of our lives, Kassie and I are finally enjoying the closeness sisters are supposed to share. We want you to be part of that. Our family isn't complete without you."

Alyssa turned to look at Kassie. She was nodding agreement.

She tried to picture what her life would be like if she stayed—working at the charter office, living in the space above, maybe even fixing it up to feel more like a home.

She would have a job, because her sisters chose to hire her. She would have a place to live, because her sisters allowed her to occupy the apartment. Everything in her life would depend on the charity of her sisters.

She didn't just want their affection. She wanted their respect. And the only way she would get it was by proving herself— being a responsible adult, standing on her own two feet, finding her own path to success.

"I'm sorry. I don't have any hard feelings. I'll stay in touch." She forced a smile. "And not just when I need to borrow money. Which I haven't forgotten about, by the way. I'm going to pay you both back for the last time as soon as I get on my feet. But leaving now...this is something I have to do."

Alyssa looked back at her plate, holding a lunch that was only half eaten. The smile she gave her sisters was much more relaxed than the last one. "But I don't have to do it before finishing this yummy lunch."

In fact, she had another hour before she would have to leave for the airport. With Peter gone and his buddies locked up, she could return to Atlanta, but she wanted her fresh start to be somewhere completely new.

So she'd continued with the airline ticket purchase she'd begun the day she'd been abducted. Different date, same destination. A little more effort had gone into her planning this time. She'd found a room to rent in the suburbs for just under a thousand per month. The first month's rent and security deposit wouldn't leave much in her checking account, but she would find a job soon.

Her living arrangements were all set. She'd already passed the background check. She'd made a lot of mistakes over the past seven years, but none of those mess-ups had impacted her adult record.

When they finished eating, Kris stacked the dishes and refused help with cleanup, insisting they weren't going to kill the last thirty minutes of their time together working in the kitchen. Instead, she led them into the family room, where two sets of French doors looked out over the backyard and Bayou Texar beyond.

Alyssa sat on the couch, and Spence eased down next to her. Apollo lay at both of their feet. Several times over the past few days, they had discussed her plans to leave. He'd said much the same things Kris had just said, that she needed the support of friends and family.

Friendship. That was all he'd offered. Not so long ago, she could have agreed. That ship had sailed. Somehow, over the past five weeks, she'd fallen right back in love with him.

Actually, the love had been there all along, stuffed beneath years of anger, resentment and rejection. He had obviously moved on when he'd made his decision to leave eight years ago. She hadn't. Seeing both of her sisters so happy had only made the ache inside even more keen.

Eventually, she would be able to think of Spence as no more than a friend, but it wouldn't happen here in Pensacola—living, sleeping and working right next door to him. No, she would have to leave.

Over the years, she'd had a handful of boyfriends. None of those relationships had worked out. She would have no reason to believe the future would be any different from the past, except from this point forward, she was going to ask God to guide her decisions. She was pretty sure that was a reasonable request. In fact, wasn't there even somewhere in the Bible that said to pray for wisdom?

As soon as everyone was seated, Bella settled down against one of the sets of French doors, and Gavin looked around the room, probably trying to decide which lap to climb into. When his eyes met Alyssa's, a smile climbed up his cheeks, and he made a beeline for her. After stepping around the dog, he held out both arms. "Issa?"

Kris corrected him. "Aunt Alyssa."

Alyssa pulled him onto her lap. "He can call me *Issa.* I kind of like it."

"If you're going to insist on leaving, you've got to at least come back for regular visits." Kris grinned. "If you do this just every seven years, Gavin is going to grow up not knowing his Auntie Issa."

Kassie nodded. "Kris is right. Let's make plans now for Christmas."

"That's less than two and a half months away. I'll be in a new job. I doubt they'll let me off."

"Okay," Kassie said. "Summer vacation."

Alyssa looked around the room, warmth filling her chest. Everyone was smiling, affection shining from their eyes. This was what family was supposed to feel like.

She hugged Gavin and shifted her gaze to the side. Spence gave the little boy some pats on the back.

Tomorrow was the grand opening of Cavanaugh Music Center. She was kind of sad she wouldn't be around to help him celebrate the realization of his dream. She should have delayed her trip by one more day.

A few minutes later, she handed Gavin off to Spence. "I'm going to order an Uber and say my goodbyes now."

Kassie frowned. "You know, any one of us would be happy to take you."

"I know, but I don't want to walk into the airport all weepy."

She stood, and the others did, too. After hugging each of her sisters, she gave their fiancés goodbye hugs. "I can't tell you how much I appreciate everything you guys have done for me—the encouragement and support, the protection detail, giving me a job and a place to stay. I promise, I'll keep in touch. And I won't stay gone so long this time."

Kassie looked at her long and hard. "It's not too late to cancel that flight."

"I have to do this."

"I understand."

She dropped to her knees for the final two hugs. Gavin wrapped his arms around her neck. "Bye, Issa."

"Bye-bye, sweetie. Auntie Issa will be back."

When Gavin released her, she looked at Apollo, who stood next to Spence, watching the activity. She patted her leg. "Come on, boy."

He trotted over to her, tail wagging, and she cupped the furry face in her hands. "I'm going to miss you, too." He responded with a slurp up one of her cheeks.

She rose to walk to the edge of the family room and then turned back around to face everyone. "Remember, this isn't *goodbye*. It's *see you later*. And *talk to you soon.* I'll let you know when I get to the place where I'll be staying."

By the time she reached the foyer, her eyes burned with unshed tears. *Get a grip.* When she'd arrived five weeks ago, she'd thought the only thing she'd feel upon leaving would be relief. With all the emotions swirling inside her, relief wasn't one of them.

She picked up her backpack from where she'd left it on the Bombay chest against the wall and then stepped onto the porch. Two rockers sat side by side. She eased into one and pulled up the Uber app on her phone.

A few minutes later, the door creaked open beside her. Her sisters and their fiancés were respecting her wishes to do this alone.

Spence wasn't. "Can I wait with you?"

She shrugged. "All right."

He sat in the rocker next to hers, and Apollo lay down in front of him. For several moments, the only sounds were the soft creaks of their chairs and the occasional rumble of a vehicle on one of the nearby roads.

Finally, Spence released a sigh. "I don't want you to leave."

"I have to."

"Why?" It was the same question her sister had asked.

"I've got to get my life on the right track, without people watching, just waiting for me to mess up. We both know that won't happen here. Our trip to Publix proved that."

"You're going to let one crotchety lady run you away from everyone who cares about you?"

"Dorothy's not the only one."

"Who else has judged you?"

"No one else has had a chance, because I haven't been out, except for Gallery Night, and everyone was too engaged with the activities to interact with me." She heaved a sigh. "Look, eight years ago, you needed your fresh start. After all this time, I finally get it. I'm not angry anymore. But now I need you to understand I need mine."

"You can have your fresh start right here. You have family who love you, a job, a place to stay until you're able to get something else." One side of his mouth cocked up in a half smile that looked more forlorn than happy. "A friend who has already proved he'll do anything to keep you safe."

And that was the problem. She didn't need another friend. Not in Spence, anyway.

"I can't make my fresh start here. I need to go somewhere where no one knows the old Alyssa, where no one will judge me for my past mistakes. Somewhere I can heal and grow and develop my newfound faith."

A Toyota Prius stopped at the curb and she stood. "Here's my ride."

He stood, too, and although she had already hugged him goodbye inside, she wrapped her arms around his neck again. His went around her and tightened. For several long moments, he didn't move. The embrace seemed to hold much more than simple friendship. But without the words to back it up, she wouldn't stay.

She released him, picked up the pack and descended the porch steps. When she had settled into the Prius's back seat, she looked toward the house. Big mistake.

Spence was standing on the porch, Apollo next to him. The dog stood stock-still, his tail not moving. Sadness seemed to fill his eyes. Was he really as upset as he looked?

When she shifted her attention to Spence, her heart squeezed. The sadness on *his* face was unmistakable. He might just as well be holding a neon sign.

The driver pulled away from the curb, and Alyssa tore her gaze from her child-hood home—and her longtime love—to stare out the front windshield.

She was doing the right thing. She'd

even prayed about it. Maybe not as seriously as she should have, but she was still pretty new to this whole prayer thing.

She wasn't the only one who needed time to heal. Spence did, too. Leaving was the right thing to do. It had to be.

So why did she feel as if she'd just left a piece of her soul on her sister's porch?

Spence sat in the wrought-iron swing, moving it in a steady back-and-forth pattern with one foot. Apollo was curled up next to him, big brown paws hanging over the front edge.

He'd left Kris's house right after Alyssa had, slipping back inside just long enough to offer quick thanks for the meal and abrupt goodbyes. He'd planned to head right to his apartment and had wound up at the park instead.

He'd asked Alyssa to stay, more than once. Each time, her answer had been the same. She needed her fresh start. He understood that part. He'd done it himself. But he'd come back.

He didn't know if Alyssa ever would. Based on what she had told him, since leaving home at eighteen, she'd lived like a vagabond, always running from the past, starting over in one place after another, searching for something she'd never been able to find.

Would her newfound faith make a difference? He hoped so. But it hadn't stopped her from leaving him.

It was all for the best, though. He needed someone stable, someone who would be there tomorrow…and the next month and next year. That wasn't Alyssa.

She needed someone stable, too. Between his nightmares and flashbacks, *stable* wasn't in his vocabulary. Throwing two messed-up people together and hoping a healthy relationship would somehow come out of the mix was being unrealistic. Two broken halves didn't make a complete whole.

Instead, he'd pray she would find a good man, someone who had his act together, someone stable enough to be her rock, whatever the future held. Someone who would strengthen her in her newfound faith, rather than lead her away.

A familiar Kia Sorento drove slowly past, Jared at the wheel. He and Kassie must have left Kris's right after he had.

Spence looked over his shoulder to watch the SUV pull into the driveway behind him. Next to him, Apollo stretched, and Spence rested his hand on his back, making slow circles in the dog's fur.

How many times had he and Alyssa sat on this same swing, talking, sharing their frustrations about their fathers, their dissatisfaction with life in general?

Before her mother had disappeared, her favorite place had been the beach. She'd practically grown up there, on weekends, anyway. Her mother had taken her and her sisters there every Saturday. When he and

Alyssa had gotten together, Spence had shared several of those outings.

Then, overnight, Alyssa had grown to hate it. He couldn't have dragged her there if he'd tried. He hadn't. He'd understood. She hadn't wanted the reminders of the mother she'd thought had deserted her. He'd been the only one in their circle of friends who hadn't tried to drag her there with them.

Instead, the two of them had made their round of all the parks in Pensacola. It had been quite a feat, considering there were more than ninety. They'd made a game of it, making a list and checking them off one by one, keeping track of their favorites. This one at North Hill was near the top.

Two paths ran diagonally from corner to corner, creating a large X, a raised bed at the intersection. A playground occupied one end of the park, a gazebo the other. Besides the swing, there were several benches placed in various locations.

Footsteps sounded against the concrete path behind him. A lone adult, judging from the sound. There was something else, too—the soft jingle of ID and rabies tags. Someone was probably walking their dog. Hopefully, the visitor would continue on past. Spence was enjoying the solitude.

The footsteps fell silent and he turned. It was Jared. He had stepped off the path and was moving toward the swing.

Jared smiled. "I thought that was you I saw sitting here."

Apollo jumped down and approached Jared and Justice, tail wagging. Jared knelt to greet the dog with some scratches on the head. When he straightened, Apollo turned to sniff Justice.

Jared walked to the swing. "Do you think Apollo will mind if I take his spot?"

"If he does, he'll get over it. Have a seat." So much for solitude. It probably wasn't the best thing for him right now, anyway.

Jared eased down next to him. "I was really hoping Alyssa was going to stay.

Kassie and Kris have been trying to persuade her for the past week."

"Yeah, me, too." His gaze drifted to the round raised bed with its knee-high brick wall, shrubs surrounding the light post rising from the center. The bulb wouldn't come on for several hours yet. Long before then, he and Apollo would be back home in the apartment. Alone.

"Are you okay with her leaving?"

Jared's words jarred Spence from his thoughts. He shrugged. "Not really."

"Then why are you here instead of at the airport?"

"Because if I throw her over my shoulder and forcibly carry her out, I'll probably be arrested."

"Words can be more persuasive than brute force."

"I already tried words. They didn't work."

"How hard did you try? I don't know what you might have said when you followed her out, but throughout the meal and afterward, you weren't exactly acting like she was worth fighting for."

He looked at Jared with raised eyebrows. They didn't even know each other that well. Maybe Jared thought his position as Alyssa's future brother-in-law entitled him to ignore social boundaries.

Jared sighed. "Look, I'm not trying to butt into your business, but I can tell you care for her. I know she cares for you, too."

"We had something years ago. We were both so messed up, what we had wasn't very healthy."

"Do you believe people can change?"

"Of course I do."

"From the little bit Kassie and Kris have said, you certainly have. I gather that Alyssa has, too."

Spence shook his head. "She needs somebody stable."

"And you're not? Let's see. You spent however many years serving your country. You're a few hours away from opening your own music store. You've got what I believe is a strong relationship with God. How much more stability do you think Alyssa needs?"

Spence heaved a sigh. Jared didn't know about all the times he awoke during the night with a scream clawing its way up his throat. Or all the seemingly innocuous things that were triggers for him: crowds, fireworks, shootouts on TV, and sometimes absolutely nothing.

He shifted his gaze to Apollo, who was currently following Justice around the park. "See the vest Apollo's wearing? Do you know what kind of service he provides?"

Jared shrugged. "I'm guessing you saw some stuff that would mess with anybody's mind and he helps you keep it all together."

Spence pressed his lips into a thin line but didn't respond.

"And you think that somehow makes you unfit to be any more than a friend.

Hey, bro, we're all broken in one way or another."

Jared stood up and whistled for Justice to join him. When the dog reached his side, he stared down at Spence. "Did you tell Alyssa how you feel? How you *really* feel?"

No, he hadn't. He'd thought it would only make things more difficult for them if she suspected the depth of his feelings for her.

But Jared was right. Everyone was broken in their own way. Jesus was the only perfect man who had ever lived. Alyssa could find someone else, someone who had never experienced abuse or combat or terror. But the man still wouldn't be perfect.

And whoever this unknown man was, he couldn't possibly love Alyssa any more than Spence did.

Jared shook his head. "The way you look right now, if you don't catch her before she leaves, there's going to be a trip to California in your near future. Do yourself a favor and save some hard-earned bucks. Go see if you can stop her from getting on that plane."

Jared turned and headed back the way he had come, his German shepherd trotting beside him.

Spence watched him walk away. Alyssa had told him she finally understood why he'd had to leave all those years ago. Maybe that meant, after eight years of resentment, she had finally forgiven him. But had she come to feel for him as she once had? Or was she content to remain just friends?

There was only one way to find out.

Spence rose from the swing, and Apollo came to attention. Jared was right. He couldn't let Alyssa leave without telling her how he felt.

He jogged back to the Subaru. The airport was only fifteen minutes away. Depending on how backed up the security line was, maybe he could catch Alyssa before she got beyond where he could go.

After leaving the SUV in the parking garage, he hurried into the airport and scanned the lines of passengers waiting in the security queues. He had almost given up when people near the TSA checkpoint shifted again, offering him a brief glimpse of red hair.

His pulse kicked into high gear. "Come, Apollo."

For the next few minutes, he zigzagged through the line, offering frequent apologies. He got several questioning glances, but only two people voiced protests, which died the moment they noticed Apollo. Maybe the dog made him look a little more official.

Alyssa stepped closer to the checkpoint, one person ahead of her now. She was only about twenty feet away.

"Alyssa!" No reaction. He was close, but not close enough for her to hear him over the murmur of voices and other noises in the airport. He wound his way closer.

She handed her ticket and driver's license to the TSA agent.

"Alyssa!"

She turned, scanning the faces around her until her gaze settled on Spence.

"Spence?"

The TSA person handed back her items. "Move on through."

Instead, Alyssa stepped back and motioned the next person to go ahead of her. When she had made her way back to Spence, they both moved as far out of the line as the barrier would allow.

She looked up at him, her eyebrows drawn together in confusion. But her smile said she was happy to see him.

"What are you doing here?"

"I came to ask you to stay."

"I can't."

Yeah, he'd made the request several times, and she'd told him the same thing every time. "That's not the only reason I'm here. I came to tell you how I feel."

She tilted her head to the side. "And how is that?"

"I love you, Alyssa. I don't think I ever stopped. I can't go back to just being your friend. I've come back home, but I realize now that nowhere is home without you in my life. I need you with me, and I hope you'll give me a chance to prove I'll always be there for you, no matter what life throws our way."

Alyssa looked at him with wide eyes and a slack jaw. "But… I *have* to go. I already bought my ticket."

"Turn it in and apply the credit toward the trip I'm hoping we'll both be taking in a few months."

"What trip?"

"Anywhere you want to go…for our honeymoon, if you'll marry me."

Her mouth opened and snapped closed again. He'd apparently put her at a loss for words. Either that or she was trying to figure out the gentlest way to say no.

When he glanced around them, they had the attention of everyone in the immediate area.

He turned back to Alyssa, who hadn't said a word since his awkward proposal. Before he'd joined the army, they had both planned to marry one day. But he could have done a little better with planning the actual proposal.

"Come on, sweetheart." He forced a teasing smile. "You're not seriously going to embarrass me in front of all these people by telling me to take a hike, are you?"

She tilted her head to the side, her lips curving up in a smirk. "Have you cleared this with Apollo?"

"He's the one who suggested it."

"In that case, how can I say no?"

She wrapped her arms around his neck and stood on her tiptoes. He met her halfway.

When his lips met hers, applause broke

out around them. Yeah, they had an audience.

It didn't matter. Nothing mattered except the woman he held in his arms. He'd waited eight long years for this moment, without even knowing what he was waiting for.

Alyssa was his, now and forever. They both had healing to do. The road ahead wouldn't be without bumps. But they had love and a shared faith.

He'd thought two broken halves couldn't make a whole. He'd been wrong.

They could, as long as God was the glue binding them together.

EPILOGUE

The sun shone from a blue sky speck-
led with fluffy white clouds, and a steady
breeze blew across the soft sand. Alyssa
stood next to Spence, wearing a tea-length,
ivory-colored gown. Kassie was on Spence's other side in an identical gown except in white, Jared beyond. Kris and
Tony completed the flattened semicircle,
Kris's dress a pale lavender. The men were
dressed in suits rather than tuxedos. A dog
sat to the left of each couple, wearing a
vest and a silk bandana matching its lady's gown.

Behind the pastor, the endless expanse
of the Gulf stretched out to meet the horizon. In the middle of May, the tempera-
ture was perfect. It had warmed up from

the cooler weather of winter, but the hot stickiness of summer hadn't yet arrived.

The triple wedding had been Kassie's idea. With her and Jared planning to tie the knot in early May, and Kris and Tony planning on late May, they'd decided to settle in the middle with a double wedding, which had grown to include the third couple when Alyssa and Spence got engaged.

It was Alyssa who had suggested involving the dogs. Spence was rarely separated from Apollo, and although the nightmares and flashbacks had decreased considerably and they had all agreed on only two hundred guests, she wasn't taking any chances. Her sisters had loved the idea.

Alyssa couldn't remember who had suggested the venue, but she had thought it was perfect. They were at Langdon Beach, part of the Gulf Islands National Seashore, one of their mother's favorite places.

They'd already said their vows and exchanged rings. Gavin had carried Kris's and Tony's forward on a silk pillow and then had taken a seat with Brandi in the front row. Even as well-behaved as he was, everyone involved had decided that, at three years old, forty minutes was a little too long to expect him to stand still.

At the moment, the pastor was charging the six of them to remember the commitment they were making today and to take it seriously, that marriage was harder than people expected.

Behind them, friends and family occupied the white folding chairs lined up on the beach. One of those family members was Spence's father. Shortly after she had decided to stay, Spence had finally given in to the nudge he had tried to ignore for several months. He'd shown up on his father's doorstep one afternoon for what would be the first of many visits.

Alyssa had had mixed feelings about opening those doors. Spence's reconciling with his father had put even more pressure on her to go see hers. Now she was glad she had. His tears and heartfelt apologies had gone a long way in allowing her to let go of the anger and resentment she had carried for so many years.

A week after that visit, he'd succumbed to the cancer ravishing his body. It was as if he'd been hanging on just long enough to make amends with his last daughter.

The pastor ended with a prayer, and a guitarist and soloist stepped forward. Gary and James were both part of the worship team at church. So was Spence. He'd volunteered shortly after arriving back in Pensacola and had been playing with them ever since.

Gary strummed an intro, and James began to sing "I Will Be Here" by Steven Curtis Chapman. Each couple had chosen a song for the wedding. This last one was Spence and Alyssa's.

As James sang, Spence squeezed Alyssa's hand, silently affirming the words of the song. It was his promise to her. She had no doubt—through the good times and bad, through the years, whatever the future held, he would be there.

When the final strains of the song had faded, the pastor prayed a blessing over all three couples and pronounced them husband and wife. "Gentlemen, you may kiss your brides."

Alyssa looked at Spence, head tilted back. Seven months had passed since he had chased her down at the airport, and she still had those occasional moments when she was afraid she was going to wake up back in Atlanta and realize this was all a dream.

Guests applauded, and she pulled away to smile at those gathered. She was now Mrs. Spencer Cavanaugh. Joy coursed through her, along with an overwhelming sense of gratitude.

She wouldn't change a thing. If things hadn't gone the way they had with Peter, she wouldn't have stayed in Pensacola for more than one night. She would have been gone before Spence arrived. She would have had no need for protection. She wouldn't have ended up living right next door to him, and there would have been no middle-of-the-night talks. Those three weeks had been some of the worst weeks of her life, but since that was what had led her to where she was now, everything she had gone through was a blessing.

A recording of "The Wedding March" played through the speaker system, and Alyssa and Spence walked down the center aisle arm in arm, Apollo trailing behind them. Kassie and Jared followed with Justice, and Kris, Tony and Bella brought up the rear, Gavin in Tony's arms.

A tent stood nearby, tables and chairs beneath. A balloon arch formed a backdrop for the head table, where six places were set, a floral centerpiece in front of each pair of chairs. Pleasant aromas drifted to them from a row of tables holding chafing dishes filled with baked chicken, scalloped potatoes and broccoli in cheese sauce.

Alyssa and Spence stopped at the edge of the tent. The others, along with the dogs, fell in next to them, forming the receiving line.

When Spence's father reached them,

he greeted Alyssa with a hug and Spence with a handshake and a smile. After stepping in front of Apollo, he bent over and held out a hand. The dog lifted a paw, and Spence's dad shook it. When he straightened, he was smiling even more broadly. The man had changed a lot over the past few months, becoming a true father to both her and Spence. He was even attending church with them on a regular basis.

Once the last guest had finished congratulating them and stepped under the tent, Spence pulled Alyssa more tightly against his side. "Not a bad ending for a proposal that took place in the security queue at the airport."

Kris grinned. "You did better than this guy." She poked Tony in the ribs with an elbow. "He proposed in a cemetery."

Tony frowned. "Not *in* a cemetery. Right *outside* the cemetery. There's a difference."

Jared laughed. "Looks like I'm the only one who did it right, with a romantic lunch on the water and a ring purchased in advance."

"But we made up for it," Tony said.

Spence nodded. "We sure did. Fancy candlelight dinner, music, the whole shebang."

As they made their way to the buffet, Alyssa looked around at those gathered. They were here for Kassie and Kris, but they were here for her, too. She smiled at her sisters, her nephew whom she'd waited far too long to get to know and the two men who had just become family. Finally, her gaze went to Spence.

Warmth flooded her. This was contentment.

From the time she'd left home seven years ago, she had searched for a new beginning, starting over in one place after another.

But all along, her new beginning was right here.

At home.

* * * * *

Dear Reader,

I hope you've enjoyed Alyssa and Spence's story. This is the third book in the Canine Defense series set in Pensacola, Florida.

We got to know Alyssa in the prior two books as the troubled younger sister who had never found a way past the traumas in her life. Spence had dealt with his own troubles, compounded by the PTSD he carried home from his time in combat. It was fun bringing these two characters with so much baggage back together and watching them let go of the past and find healing. They both learned that God really does make all things new if we let Him.

Be on the lookout for more books in the Canine Defense series. May God richly bless you in all you do.

Love in Christ,
Carol J. Post